"I'M NOT SAYING YOU'RE _____
said. "You're going thro_____
ing to help you—from t_____ of someone
who's been there."

"Why? No, don't answer that."

"Why not? Are you afraid of the answer?"

"No! I'm not afraid of anything."

"If it helps, I'm afraid too," he said. He brushed
a strand of her hair behind her ear. "I guess it's like
falling off a horse."

She shook her head in denial. "That's an idiotic
comparison."

"Is it? The longer I wait, the harder it gets."

That did it. So, she was his testing ground?

"You're so damn eager to get back in the race?
Fine. I'll give you a leg up." She grasped his shoulders, squeezed her eyes shut, and clamped her lips
on his.

He was frozen at first, with pure shock, but
within a split second he responded with instinctual
heat. His mouth moved, taking command. What
had started as a lesson to be taught turned quickly
into something Millicent hadn't bargained for.

For a few seconds she let her own instincts conquer everything else. She opened her mouth against
his, tasting him, reveling in the fire and the smoky
heat of their mingled desire. The last rays of the
dying sun peeked through the trees, spotlighting
their moment of passion.

WHAT ARE *LOVESWEPT* ROMANCES?

They are stories of true romance and touching emotion. We believe those two very important ingredients are constants in our highly sensual and very believable stories in the LOVESWEPT line. Our goal is to give you, the reader, stories of consistently high quality that may sometimes make you laugh, sometimes make you cry, but are always fresh and creative and contain many delightful surprises within their pages.

Most romance fans read an enormous number of books. Those they truly love, they keep. Others may be traded with friends and soon forgotten. We hope that each LOVESWEPT romance will be a treasure—a "keeper." We will always try to publish

LOVE STORIES YOU'LL NEVER FORGET
BY AUTHORS YOU'LL ALWAYS REMEMBER

The Editors

Loveswept ® 839

BRIDES OF DESTINY: MILLICENT'S MEDICINE MAN

KAREN LEABO

BANTAM BOOKS
NEW YORK · TORONTO · LONDON · SYDNEY · AUCKLAND

BRIDES OF DESTINY: MILLICENT'S MEDICINE MAN

A Bantam Book / June 1997

ISBN 0-553-44545-6

Published simultaneously in the United States and Canada

---

*Bantam Books are published by Bantam Books, a division of Bantam
Doubleday Dell Publishing Group, Inc. Its trademark, consisting of the
words "Bantam Books" and the portrayal of a rooster, is Registered in
U.S. Patent and Trademark Office and in other countries. Marca Regis-
trada. Bantam Books, 1540 Broadway, New York, New York 10036.*

PRINTED IN THE UNITED STATES OF AMERICA

OPM   10 9 8 7 6 5 4 3 2 1

AUTHOR'S NOTE

Hard to believe it's been fourteen years since Loveswept first arrived on the romance novel scene. Let's see, that would make it 1983? I would have been still in grammar school! (That's a joke. I won't tell you how old I was, but I was plenty old enough to enjoy those first Loveswepts!)

No one can say Loveswept didn't know how to pick its debut authors. Every one of those first six authors—Sandra Brown, Helen Mittermeyer, Noelle Berry McCue, Fayrene Preston, Carla Neggers, and Dorothy Garlock—have become household words among romance fans. I feel honored to be following in their footsteps, and very excited to be included in Loveswept's Fourteenth Anniversary Celebration.

When I first discovered Loveswept I was just starting out as an aspiring novelist. I submitted several manuscripts to Loveswept's editors; all of them were rejected. Looking back, those rejection slips were blessings in disguise. If any of those early efforts had actually been published, I'm afraid to think what would have happened to my writing career!

I ended up selling to another publisher, but I always kept my eye on Loveswept. Whether the books were about a spy and a princess or the boy and girl next door, written with wacky humor or poignant, heartrending emotion, there was (and is) a certain boldness to this line that always appealed to me. The books were anything but predictable.

In the back of my mind, I kept thinking that, since my own stories are sometimes risky and challenging (or quirky and off-the-wall, depending on who you ask), I could be a Loveswept author. Last year that dream came true for me, with the publication of *Hell On Wheels*, my first Loveswept.

Millicent's Medicine Man is the third story in a trilogy about three high school friends from Destiny, Texas, who share a spooky experience, and whose futures are intertwined. The focus of the story is on children—seven in all—which made it fun to write. I don't have children of my own, but I certainly enjoyed them vicariously through the adventures of Millicent and her doctor hero, Jase.

I hope you enjoy *Millicent's Medicine Man* and

that you'll keep reading Loveswept. The names on the covers change over the years, but the books will always sweep you away!

Karen Leabo

PROLOGUE

Ten Years Ago

A bead of perspiration rolled down eighteen-year-old Millicent Whitney's forehead, between her eyebrows, and down her upturned nose. She longed to wipe it away, but her hands were full. With her right hand she was painting an intricate unicorn. She used her left to steady the head of a four-year-old girl, whose cheek was Millicent's canvas.

It was carnival time again at Destiny High School, and Millicent had been rooked into working the face-painting booth again, the way she was every year.

She didn't really mind. The job allowed her contact with children, which she loved, and gave her a safe haven to return to if she started feeling overwhelmed. She had actually wandered around a bit that morning when it wasn't so crowded and played a few of the games. One of the boys at the goldfish booth had flirted with her, and she now had a new pet thanks to her foolish attempts to prolong the contact and the giddy feeling his teasing had given her, even if she hadn't flirted back.

"What did the princess see?" the little girl asked.

Millicent had gotten distracted from her fairy tale by her own musings for a moment, but the child's question brought her back. "See for yourself," she said as she put the finishing touches on the unicorn, then handed the girl a "magic looking glass."

The girl squealed in delight. "A oonicorn!"

"And when she jumped on the unicorn's back, the evil spell cast by the witch was broken, and the princess rode back to her castle. Her mother and father, the queen and king, welcomed her home, and they had a great feast to celebrate."

"With cotton candy?" the child asked hopefully.

Millicent winced as she thought of what that sticky stuff would do to her masterpiece. "Yes, I think that's what the princess asked for." She lifted the little girl from her high stool and set her on the ground with a pat. The girl went running to her father, who'd been looking on.

"Very nice," the father said. "You have a lot of talent."

Millicent felt herself blushing. She tried for a reply, but the man and his daughter walked away before she could form one.

She was about to kick herself for being so socially inept when she spied Callie Calloway and Lana Walsh heading resolutely in her direction, and some of her irritation seeped away. The three girls had worked together on the Carnival Committee for months, and Millicent felt she could actually call them her friends now.

Imagine, shy, mousy Millicent Whitney being friends with two of the most popular girls at Destiny High. She'd been terrified when she'd first found out who was on the committee with her. She'd assumed the other two girls would shut her out or make fun of her ideas. But she'd soon found out they weren't much different from her. They were both a little shy at first, a little uneasy, and then suddenly they'd been blurting out excited ideas and scribbling lists and volunteering for various tasks.

She'd had more fun working with them than she had during her entire high school career.

"Hi, how's it going?" Millicent found it easy to talk with the few people she knew well.

"Fine with me," Lana said, flipping a lock of her golden hair behind her ear, "but Callie says we have official business to take care of."

Millicent looked to Callie for clarification.

Callie turned and pointed to the corner of the gym, where a red-silk-swathed booth glittered invitingly. "Did y'all see that?"

Millicent felt a small jolt of awareness, a tingling up her spine. She'd never seen that booth before. How could she have missed it? The small booth featured a gold-lettered sign that read, "Theodora, Fortuneteller."

"The fortuneteller?" Millicent said, consciously making her words sound casual. "What about her?"

"She's not on the list. Where'd she come from?" Callie asked.

The two other girls shrugged. "Does it matter?" Millicent asked, even though her instincts were telling her it mattered a great deal.

"Of course it matters. She might have sneaked in here under false pretenses. She might be taking cash under the table."

"Callie, you're so suspicious," Lana scolded gently. "Maybe Mr. Stipley forgot to tell us about her." Mr. Stipley was the principal of Destiny High School, and the carnival was his baby.

"I want to find out for sure," Callie said. "And I want you both to come with me."

Lana laughed. "All right. But if we find out she's legit, we all have to have our fortunes told. Agreed?"

Callie nodded reluctantly, and Millicent, not wanting to be a party pooper, followed suit, though anything that smacked of fortunetelling scared her a little. She wasn't sure that humans were meant to see across the dark curtain to the other side.

"Theodora" sat behind a silk-draped table with a crystal ball in front of her, as if she'd been waiting for these three customers. She looked convincingly gypsyish in a peasant blouse and multicolored tiered skirt, bangles on her wrist, and a scarf covering her thick black hair.

She smiled warmly at the trio. "Well, now, what do we have here? Did you come to find out which boy will ask you to the prom?"

No, Millicent thought with a flash of irritation. Why validate the bad news she already knew was true?

"Actually, Miss, uh, Ms. Theodora, this is an official visit," Callie said. "I'm head of the Carnival Committee's student division, and these are my committee members." She pushed her wire-rimmed glasses to the bridge of her nose and consulted her clipboard. "You aren't on my list."

"My, aren't you the official one," Theodora said, still smiling. To Lana and Millicent she added in a loud stage whisper, "I'll bet nothing gets by this one, eh? She probably dots all her i's and crosses the t's."

Millicent covered her mouth to disguise her smile, and Lana laughed out loud, stopping only when Callie scowled at her.

"You're the skeptical type," Theodora continued, looking at Callie. "You love to ask questions and you can't stand an unsolved mystery. You would make a very good newspaper reporter."

"H-how did you know that?" Callie asked.

Millicent felt that quiver of uneasiness again. How did this woman, this stranger, know that Callie was planning to study journalism at Stockton University?

"I know all kinds of things," Theodora said, wiggling her eyebrows mysteriously. "Would you like to hear more?"

"I'd like to hear who gave you permission to set up here," Callie persisted, using that "official" voice that sounded so adult to Millicent. "You're not on my—"

"Chill out, Callie," Lana said. "I'd like to hear more. Can you tell me who I'll go to the prom with?"

Theodora gazed into her crystal ball, while Callie pulled a small pad and pen from the back pocket of her jeans. "I see you going to the prom with a football player," Theodora said.

Lana sighed with obvious delight, while Callie rolled her eyes. Callie, of course, wasn't being taken in, Millicent thought.

Theodora looked up at Lana. "You have many talents, you know," she said. "I see you surrounded by flowers."

Lana giggled. "I hope that means Bart will bring me a big ol' corsage for the dance. Now, what about Millicent?"

Much to Millicent's discomfort, Lana grabbed her by the wrist and pulled her forward. "Who's she gonna go with?"

Millicent sighed. She'd have just as soon foregone this humiliation. "I don't need a fortuneteller to give me that answer. I won't be going." Who would ask her? The boy at the goldfish booth? She didn't even know his name. She hadn't been brave enough to introduce herself.

Theodora peered into the ball. "I see you painting. You have such talent!"

"I'll probably be painting the prom decorations," Millicent said wistfully.

"Oh, who cares about this silly prom business," Lana interrupted hastily, perhaps sensing her friend's discomfort. Lana was good about that. "We want to know who we're going to marry. Right?" She looked to the other two girls for confirmation.

"Gee, I'm not sure I want to know. . . ." Millicent said, but Theodora was already staring into her crystal ball.

The gypsy was quiet for a long time while the girls waited nervously. Then, to Millicent's increasing unease, Theodora looked up and recited a poem:

> One will tarry, losing her chance at love
> The next will marry, but her spouse will rove
> A third will bury her man in a hickory grove
> But all will find marriage a treasure trove
> With a little help from above

Millicent took an instinctive step backward. There was something really spooky about Theodora, something otherworldly. Her fortuneteller act went beyond a flashy costume and clever patter. Millicent suddenly believed, with all her heart, that this woman could see things other people couldn't.

And Millicent knew which line of the poem was meant for her. Even if she did manage to find a husband someday, she doubted she had the where-withal to hold on to a man. He would be the one to "rove."

"The poem's nice, but it's not very helpful," Lana pointed out. "I want a name. How will I know my future husband when I meet him?"

Theodora smiled. "No problem. Everyone who has her fortune told by Theodora gets a souvenir. These mementos will help you recognize the man who will make you happy." She reached under the table and pulled out a cardboard box, which appeared to be filled with gum machine toys and other plastic junk. She rummaged around in it for a moment, then held out her hand toward Callie.

Callie, her expression still filled with skepticism, nonetheless reached out and accepted Theodora's gift. It was a plastic key chain in the shape of a cowboy boot.

Millicent felt that chill again. How did Theodora know about Sam, Callie's on-again, off-again boyfriend who did rodeo and wanted to be a rancher?

"I'm not marrying anyone who wears cowboy boots," Callie said, folding her arms. Theodora merely gave her a knowing smile.

Lana looked a little frightened as Theodora handed her a toy policeman's badge. She studied it, obviously perplexed.

Millicent's heart beat wildly as Theodora

searched for what seemed like an hour. She was beginning to believe there wasn't a trinket for her, that her situation was completely hopeless. But finally Theodora came up with a small bottle made of brown glass. The raised letters on the bottle read, "Dr. Desmond's Stomach Bitters."

What, I'm going to marry a hypochondriac? Millicent thought.

As the three girls studied their gifts, Theodora quietly stood and walked to the back of her booth.

"Hey, where'd she go?" Callie asked.

Lana pointed to the wavering curtain in the rear of the booth. "Back there."

Callie lunged forward, with Lana hot on her heels, and Millicent close behind. Callie pulled back the curtain, but no one was there.

The girls stepped outside the booth, looked around corners, under tables. There was no glimpse of Theodora.

"This way!" Callie suddenly said, pointing toward the back door of the gym. They all three took off at a run in hot pursuit of the fortuneteller. But outside they found no sign of her.

"I knew it," Callie said, gasping for breath, more from fear than exertion. "I knew she was some kind of charlatan."

"I didn't think she was so bad," Lana said. "She told our fortunes for free."

"We'll have to go to Mr. Stipley," Callie said. "Something's definitely fishy."

They went back into the gymnasium, but almost

before the door slammed behind them, Callie skidded to a stop so suddenly that Lana ran into her and Millicent did the same, like three bumper cars.

"Look," Callie whispered. She pointed toward Theodora's booth—or rather, the place where Theodora's booth had stood a minute or two earlier. Now there was no sign of red silk or glitter. A dart game occupied the space. There was no way anyone could have moved Theodora's booth that quickly.

The three girls stared at each other, and an almost overwhelming sense of *knowing* swept over Millicent. The three of them had experienced something important, and Millicent couldn't help feeling that it would change their lives somehow.

"D-did we just have a group hallucination?" Millicent said, her voice sounding even more tentative than usual. She still clutched the antique medicine bottle in her hand, so that part, at least, was real.

She saw that her friends still had their trinkets too.

"I'm not sure what it was," Callie said. "But I don't think we should tell anyone about it."

"Agreed," the other two girls said together. They all shook hands on the deal. Millicent felt a weird vibration coursing through their clasped hands, as if some unseen force had cemented their agreement.

ONE

They were in for another storm.

It was late March, and already Destiny, Texas, had seen a tornado wipe out the Mini-Storage lot and high winds take off the roof of the First Baptist Church.

Millicent Jones kept an uneasy watch out the kitchen window as she finished up the dinner dishes. It wasn't that storms scared her. She'd grown up with them; spring in central Texas meant thunderstorms, and that was that. But at this stage in her pregnancy, every aspect of life took on new meaning. Every danger seemed magnified right along with all of her unpredictable emotions.

Out in the boonies where she lived, far from city services, storms offered special hazards to a woman living alone with her three small children. A woman who was so huge and unwieldy that she could barely make it across a room, much less to the storm cellar.

No rain had fallen yet, but blue-black cumulus clouds were building on the horizon, so close, Millicent thought she could walk outside and touch them. Jagged lightning bolts jumped from cloud to cloud, sometimes reaching for the ground with sharp cracks of electricity. The air, even inside her kitchen, felt heavy and forbidding.

"Mama, I'm a-scared of the sto-rum." Lily, Millicent's three-year-old, clung to her mother's leg with uncharacteristic timidity. "Pick me up?"

"She can't pick you up, dodo bird," said Will, who'd just turned eight, as he careered into the kitchen. "The doctor said she can't lift heavy weights, and you weigh a ton."

"Do not!" Lily said, her lower lip jutting out.

"Will, don't call your sister names," Millicent interceded. "Tell her you're sorry."

"I'm sorry she's a dodo bird."

"Will!"

"Okay, okay." The boy bent down to three-year-old level. "Sorry, Lily. You're not a dodo bird and you don't weigh a ton. But don't bug Mom about picking you up. She's already carrying around an extra fifty pounds." He gave Millicent's tummy a cautious pat.

"Only thirty-five," Millicent retorted with mock indignation, although it did feel like fifty.

Another crack of thunder, closer this time, shook the house. Lily squealed and hid her face against Millicent's leg. "C'mon, Lil," Millicent said, ruffling her daughter's crop of curly blond hair, a legacy from her father. Her other two kids had her own plain-Jane straight brown hair. "Let's go out on the screen porch and keep an eye on that nasty ol' storm so it won't take us by surprise."

"Hey, Mom, is there any dessert?" Will asked, apparently unconcerned about the thunder and lightning.

"There's pudding in the fridge. Leave some for the rest of us," Millicent answered as she took Lily's hand and led her out of the kitchen, through the living room, and out the front door to the huge screened-in porch. Ronnie had added on the porch to their little country house with his own two hands. He'd also added on two bedrooms and an extra bath, seamlessly blending the new architecture with the old so that the house was not so little anymore.

But sometimes it still felt as if the walls could close in on Millicent.

As she passed through the living room she heard the comforting sound of Nancy, her oldest at almost ten, practicing her viola. Obviously the storm wasn't bothering Nancy either.

Millicent settled onto the porch swing with Lily nestled under her arm. There was no room in her lap, but they could still snuggle.

"Is it gonna rain?" Lily asked.

"Probably. The rain is good for our garden." If the whole thing, newly planted, didn't wash away. She could see the rain approaching in a great, blue-gray wall.

"What if lightning hits the house?"

"We'll hear a big boom, and the lights might go out. But we have candles and flashlights." Could she remember where the flashlight was? Did it have batteries? So many things to remember, things Ronnie would have taken care of if he were there.

Another clap of thunder punctuated her sentence, loud enough to shake the house. Lily squealed again. A gust of wind caused a loose piece of screening to flap wildly. The smell of approaching rain, normally welcome in drought-prone Destiny, now carried menace.

Two lightning bolts struck almost simultaneously, creating deafening booms in quick succession. The trees in the front yard swayed violently with the wind, some bending almost to the ground. Then a third bolt reached out of the sky, turning Lily's fears into reality. It struck the house with a crash that made Millicent's ears ring. Lily screamed, and Millicent's heart beat frantically. What was that smell? Was it just the ozone, or . . .

Dear God, the house was on fire.

Millicent sprang into action. She leaped for the front door with an agility she hadn't demonstrated in months and tore it open. "Will! Nancy!" she hollered. "Call nine-one-one. The house is on—"

Her two older children were already on their way. They burst into the living room from two different directions. "Mom, I already tried," Nancy said, her eyes as big as saucers. "The phone is dead."

"Grab my purse, it's got the cellular inside," Millicent ordered with the authority of a general in the midst of battle. "Then take Lily and get outside. Don't stop for anything. I'll get busy with the hose."

She turned, knowing her directions would be followed. Her two older children had become extremely responsible since their father's death, sometimes almost too adultlike in their actions and their solemn faces.

She sprinted across the porch to the outer door, her mind on logistics. First determine where the fire was. Figure out which hose was closest—Ronnie, a fireman, had been fanatic about hoses, and there were three in good working order—then put out the fire.

Simple. Except that Millicent was so intent on her mission that she didn't pay close enough attention to where her feet were landing on the wooden porch stairs. A sudden gust of wind caught her off balance; her right foot flew out from underneath her, and she fell backward. Her rear hit with jarring contact, followed by her back. Then her head snapped, striking the sharp corner of the top stair.

She was so stunned, she couldn't even cry out. A sharp pain tore through her abdomen. Then . . . blackness.

Jase Desmond looked at his watch and cursed. Eight minutes since that terrified little girl had placed the 9-1-1 call. Eight minutes, and the chopper still wasn't airborne.

Apparently it wasn't going to be. "We can't put her up," the pilot announced over the radio. "The wind . . ."

"Let's get an ambulance going, then," Jase announced. He was the senior physician on duty in the E.R. that evening, and every nurse and paramedic in the place jumped at his harshly delivered order.

"Dispatch called again," said the E.R. switchboard operator. "The little girl said she thinks her mother is in labor."

Jase cursed. What else could go wrong? "Where's Don Lumn?"

"Delivery room. Emergency cesarean in progress."

"Damn! I'm going."

"But—"

"I don't have any choice." Jase was already heading for the exit marked Emergency Personnel Only. Outside, he met up with Kathy Cedric, an O.B. nurse he'd drafted for the trip out to Willow Lake, an unincorporated slice of pure country on the outskirts of Destiny. The ambulance pulled up. He vaulted into the back with her.

Kathy, her corkscrew black hair curling every which way in the humidity, looked questioningly at him as the ambulance took off with a lurch, siren screaming.

"The woman is in labor," he said to explain his

presence. "We may be delivering a baby. I'm not an obstetrician, of course—"

"Dr. Desmond, please, you don't have to qualify yourself to me. I'm thrilled to have you here. We're a little shorthanded, what with that pileup on the interstate. If we have to deliver a baby . . . well, you've certainly handled your share of newborns."

That was true. As a pediatric neurologist, his patients were often preemies. He'd spent plenty of hours in delivery rooms monitoring fetal brain waves, so he was familiar enough with birthing procedures. But he'd never delivered a baby on his own, had never even seen one delivered outside of the sterile hospital walls.

Heavy rains hampered the ambulance's progress. Twice the dispatch operator patched through a call from the little girl—her name was Nancy—and Jase gave her instructions.

"Shouldn't I move her?" Nancy asked in a remarkably calm, rational voice. "She's lying on the stairs."

"No. She shouldn't be moved. I know she's probably uncomfortable, but—"

"But what about the fire?"

"The *what?*" No one had told him about a fire.

"It's just a little corner of the porch, but it's getting bigger."

"In this rain?"

"It's not raining here, just blowing."

"You'll have to use your own judgment, sweetheart." Jase thought about his own ten-year-old daughter, and how she would react in a situation like this. Probably not nearly as well as Nancy. "If you feel your mother is in danger from the fire, you'll have to move her."

"Okay. Oh, I think it's raining. Yes, I felt a drop! Hurry, won't you please?"

"We're about five or ten minutes away at the most. Hang on, Nancy."

The ambulance turned onto a dirt road and began to bounce and buck like a rodeo bull. The driver swerved to avoid one rain-filled pothole after another. He missed the turn onto the property the first time they passed, wasting valuable time. Finally he found it. An ancient wooden bridge that spanned a rain-swelled creek groaned in protest as the ambulance rolled over it.

A fire engine from the volunteer fire department of Crumley, the nearest town besides Destiny, was already there, but appeared to be unneeded. Rain was falling in sheets now, and there were no flames in sight.

Jase lunged for the rear doors almost before the ambulance had lurched to a stop beside the sprawling one-story house. His rubber-soled shoes made a squishing noise as he landed in the wet grass. Kathy and the other paramedic were right behind him with the gurney.

"She's right here, Doc," a fireman in a black rubber coat yelled, motioning.

Jase took in the scene—the young girl standing by the screened-in porch, looking like a drowned kitten. Two firemen talking to two younger children, drying them off with towels while trying to shelter them beneath a raincoat. Finally, Jase's eyes were drawn to his patient's pale, oval face. That was all of her that was visible. The rest of her was beneath what looked like a pile of blankets and a plastic tarp.

Her eyes fluttered open as he drew near. Good, the doctor in him thought. She's conscious. *Good Lord*, the man in him thought. She had the most gorgeous, big brown eyes he'd ever seen. "Hi, I'm Jase Desmond," he said in his most reassuring bedside manner. As he spoke he took out his penlight and flickered it from one of her eyes to the other, watching with satisfaction as both pupils contracted against the narrow beam of light.

"I'm in labor," she said in a surprisingly strong voice.

"Are you sure?"

"Of course I'm sure. I've had three kids already, so I know what it feels like. This baby is about to make an appearance. So can we skip the exam and get me to the hospital?"

"We can't move you until I check for spinal injuries—"

"Look, I don't care if my back is broken, I'm not giving birth on my front porch steps."

"You've probably got hours to go yet," he soothed as he removed her shoes. "Wiggle your toes for me."

She complied. "I'm not paralyzed, believe me.

And I don't have hours to go. My kids come quick. Lily . . . took . . ." She squinched her eyes closed, her face wracked with pain, but she made no sound. The moment passed. "Lily took less than two hours."

"She's right," Kathy said in an undertone. "This is Millicent Jones, and I've helped deliver two of her kids. She pops 'em right out."

"The pains are coming pretty fast," said the little girl, Nancy, who'd been watching solemnly from the sidelines. She held a chrome Timex watch in her hands. "That one was less than two minutes from the one before."

Two minutes! "Okay, let's move her," Jase said. A cervical board was already in place beside the stairs. "Clear the way, please." The firemen and children stood back. Jase took his place by Millicent Jones's shoulder while the others found their spots. "On three. One, two . . ." They lifted her smoothly onto the cervical board, positioning her head in a foam brace.

The gurney nearly flew into the ambulance by itself. "My kids!" Millicent objected. "Who's going to watch them? They'll have to come along."

"I'm here," a new voice piped in. Jase spared a glance toward the newcomer, a petite blond woman. With a start he realized he recognized her. She'd brought her son into the E.R. a few months earlier with a minor head injury.

"Lana?" Millicent said.

"I'm here, Millie," Lana said. "Nancy called me

when she couldn't get hold of your parents. Sloan's here too. We'll make sure the house is secure, then we'll bring the kids on to the hospital."

"Sounds like your daughter has a good head on her shoulders," Jase commented as they loaded the stretcher into the ambulance. "She thought of everything."

"She's a good girl. You kids mind Mrs. Gaston, now," Millicent called. The ambulance doors cut off the last of her warning.

"Get those wet clothes off of her," Jase ordered, now all business.

Millicent hissed as another contraction hit. Kathy comforted her patient until the pain subsided, then applied a pair of scissors to Millicent's sweater, then her pants.

"Darn, that was my favorite sweater too," she said wistfully.

Lord spare him from women and their clothes concerns! Jase thought, averting his eyes until Kathy had the woman properly draped. She was having a baby, and she was worried about a sweater? Then again, he had to admire her calmness. Libby had always gone into hysterics during labor.

Jase busied himself scrubbing his hands and arms with a sterile cleansing solution. Despite Kathy's warning, he didn't really believe he would have to deliver the baby. Another fifteen minutes, and they'd be back at Methodist and Don Lumn could take over.

Jase almost lost his footing as the ambulance

veered and bounced along the dirt drive. Abruptly its progress halted. "Jay-*sus*," the driver said.

"What?" Jase peered forward. What he saw required no explanations. The bridge they'd crossed just minutes before was now a yawning chasm of swollen creek. "Ah, hell."

"What?" Millicent asked, her voice tinged with apprehension.

"The bridge is washed out," Jase explained, as matter-of-factly as he dared. "Is there another way out of here?"

Millicent tried to sit up, but Jase stopped her with a hand to her shoulder. "Don't you dare move. You can point."

"My back is okay, honest," she said. "I'd really prefer to be sitting up. I've never given birth flat on my back."

"You're going to this time," Jase said through gritted teeth. "Now, is there another way out?"

She sighed, defeated, and made do with pointing and gesturing. "If you can cross the pasture behind the house, on the far side it meets up with James Pierce Road. There's no fence. Turn right and—uh—ah—"

Another contraction? Surely it hadn't been even a minute since the last one. "You got that?" Jase asked the driver.

"I'll give it a shot, but this ain't no off-road vehicle, you know."

"Never mind," Millicent said as a preternatural

calm stole over her. "It's too late. We won't make it to the hospital."

Kathy pulled aside the sterile drape she'd placed over the patient. Her eyes widened. "She's right, Dr. Desmond. The baby is crowning."

There was no time to prep the mother or even prepare a proper reception for the baby. Millicent was seconds away from birth. She grabbed onto the edges of her stretcher, gave a couple of pushes, and the tiniest, most perfect human being Jase had ever seen fell right into his hands.

Jase's eyes locked with Millicent's, and he shared a moment so powerful, it took his breath away. So much wisdom in those brown eyes of hers, the maternal wisdom of the ages. And joy. And pain.

"You have a new daughter, Mrs. Jones," Jase said, his throat thick.

Kathy took over, obviously knowing exactly what came next. She cleaned out the baby's mouth, then placed her tummy down on Millicent's abdomen.

"We reached the road," the driver called out. "Looks like smooth sailing from here."

As if to celebrate the good news in her own way, the baby cried, a thin mewl at first, then an all-out bawling. Millicent cried too. Jase came awful damn close. He'd watched his own children being born— from a safe distance—but the birth of this baby inexplicably moved him.

Millicent smiled through her tears. "A daughter. I never let them tell me during the sonogram. I like to be surprised. Ronnie always said he wanted two of each, but I'm sure he'll—that he would be pleased anyway."

"Your husband," Jase said, crashing back to reality. "Has anyone notified him?"

Kathy was shaking her head frantically, but it was too late for him to take back the words. He realized immediately that he'd said something wrong when he saw the pain that flashed across Millicent's face.

"The fireman who died last year," Kathy said.

Of course. Ronnie Jones. Jase should have made the connection. A warehouse fire, late last summer, he recalled. "I'm sorry. I didn't realize—"

"It's okay," Millicent said.

"I'm sorry he couldn't be here to share this with you," he said. Guilt flashed through him as he realized he wasn't telling the total truth. If Ronnie Jones were alive, he would be the one kneeling by Millicent's stretcher, one hand on her bare shoulder, the other atop her hand, which rested on the baby's head.

"I think he knows," she said. "From somewhere. I can't believe that he simply doesn't exist anymore. He's got to be somewhere, in some form."

Jase used to believe that, too, about Libby. But that was when he was still in denial. He knew now that, for his purposes, she lived on only in the three beautiful children she'd left behind.

"It's comforting to believe that," he said.

"But not realistic?"

He shrugged. "Who's to say?" He'd stopped looking for answers to questions like that. You could drive yourself crazy. "Sometimes I wish I knew for sure, and other times I'm positive we mere mortals weren't meant to know a damn thing about why things happen." He was surprised at the note of bitterness that came out. Surely he was done with all that.

"You've lost someone, too, haven't you?" she said gently.

"Yeah. But it was a long time ago, and this is no time to get maudlin," he said sternly, more to himself than her. "This is a time of celebration. You have a new daughter. What will you name her?"

"Hmm, I haven't really decided. My oldest girl, Nancy, named the last baby. Lily. I think I'll let my son have a crack at this one."

"You're a trusting soul. Are you sure you want to do that? You might end up with a daughter named after a superhero or a video game."

"Will does love his comic books. Spidermanda Jones. Has a nice ring." Millicent laughed, then stopped abruptly, one protective hand holding the baby close. "Oh, ouch, I shouldn't do that. Hey, maybe I should name the baby after you, since you delivered her. What's your name again?"

"Desmond. Jase, short for Jason. I don't think you should stick a little girl with either of those names."

Millicent stared at him. "Desmond? Really? What an odd coincidence."

"How so?"

She didn't answer him. She abruptly closed off by staring up at the roof of the ambulance. He was curious, but he didn't ask her again. He figured she would tell him if she wanted him to know.

The trip to the hospital was blessedly quick, and Jase was all too happy to relinquish his patient to Don Lumn. Still, he felt a pang of loss as he watched Millicent and her newborn being wheeled away.

"Nice job, Dr. Desmond," Kathy said.

"Hell, I didn't do anything. That delivery was about as complicated as taking a cake out of an oven."

"I meant your bedside manner. You did a great job of keeping Mrs. Jones calm, saying all the right things."

"Oh, yeah. Asking her about her husband was a swift move."

"At first I didn't think so. Then I realized she was already thinking about him. She needed to get what she was feeling out in the open. Since you've . . ." Kathy paused, choosing her words carefully. "Since you've been through the same kind of loss, you knew the right words to say."

"Can anyone ever really say the right thing?" he asked. It was a rhetorical question.

Kathy looked perplexed, and after an awkward

silence she nodded a farewell and went back to her business.

After checking in at the E.R., where things were typically hysterical, Jase headed for the doctors' lounge, pondering why he felt so unsettled. He should be elated. He'd delivered a baby. He'd gotten Millicent Jones and her offspring to the hospital without mishap, despite a surprise fire and a washed-out bridge.

But to his dismay, his brief contact with Millicent had knocked loose some old baggage. For the first time in months he found himself thinking about Libby, evaluating how his life was progressing without her.

A couple of hours earlier, he would have answered without hesitation. *Just fine.* Now he wasn't so sure. Seeing Millicent's pain had been like looking into an old mirror.

He hadn't liked seeing her suffer. But more than that, he hadn't liked what her suffering had reminded him of. He was done with all that, dammit. Libby was ancient history. Whatever he'd done right or wrong where she was concerned didn't matter anymore.

TWO

Millicent opened her eyes after a brief nap to find Dr. Desmond's face mere inches from her own. She caught a whiff of clean, soap-scented male, something she'd been without for a long while, and a velvet knot coiled in her stomach.

She must have made a funny face, because he jumped back. "Didn't mean to startle you," he said. "You were making noises in your sleep."

"Really?" How embarrassing. "What kind of noises?"

"Distressed noises. Are you in pain?"

She shook her head. Not with all the drugs she'd been given. Since the baby wasn't breast-feeding, she was free to take something for postpartum pain. "How's the baby?" she asked, as she asked every doctor or nurse who entered her room. Dr. Desmond had been a frequent recipient of that question. He'd been hovering over her the last couple of days like a worried mother cat over a sickly kitten.

"She's doing great. After she gains another couple of ounces, we'll let her out of the incubator and she can stay here in your room with you."

"That'll be terrific. I can't wait." She'd never been separated from a newborn before. All of her other babies had been delivered with textbook perfection, eight pounds plus, bursting with health and vitality.

"Do you have a name yet?" Jase asked with what seemed more than doctorly interest.

She nodded. "Will did me proud. Mary Jane. Plain but dignified."

"Nice. Um, your son didn't happen to say where he got the idea, did he?"

"No . . . why?"

"Spiderman's wife is named Mary Jane."

Millicent said nothing for a moment. Then, "You mean my child is named for a comic book character after all?"

"Just a theory." Jase laughed, and she joined him.

"Ouch, that still hurts," she said with a hand to her abdomen.

"Sorry. I'll try not to be so amusing. Normally I'm real dull."

"I'll just bet."

"No, really." He sobered. "It's been a long time since I could laugh—almost three years, in fact."

Millicent cast her eyes down, searching for

something else to talk about. Although Dr. Desmond had made the opening, obviously inviting her to inquire further, it didn't seem appropriate to discuss something so personal with a man she hardly knew.

"I lost my wife, you know." Jase pulled a chair up to her bedside with an almost conspiratorial air.

"I heard something about that," she murmured. "It's not something you have to talk about on my account." Please, she thought, don't talk about it.

Her prayers went unanswered. "It doesn't bother me. Enough time has gone by. I'm way past being sensitive. I went through all those classic stages of grief—denial, anger, bargaining with God. If you've ever taken a psychology class, I'm sure you learned about those."

Millicent had never taken psychology. She'd dropped out of college before finishing her freshman year, when she and Ronnie had gotten married. She didn't know there were supposed to be "classic stages" of grief.

Jase Desmond was looking at her with incredibly clear, intelligent hazel eyes, waiting for her to agree. She nodded uncertainly, not wanting to appear ignorant.

"Your loss is so recent, I wouldn't be surprised if you were still angry," he said, sounding wise and confident. "It seems especially cruel that your husband was taken away before he could see his child."

Suddenly she did feel angry, but not at God or the world or fate or at Ronnie himself for leaving her in such a pickle. She was angry at this man who was less than a stranger but certainly not a friend, for intruding where he didn't belong.

"You know something?" she said, folding her arms defensively. "This is really none of your business. Just because you saw me naked—"

"Wait, wait, wait." He formed his hands into a time-out sign. "This has nothing to do with the fact that I delivered your baby. I just thought that since I've been through what you're going through—"

"I'm sure it's nothing the same!"

"It's bound to be something the same," he argued good-naturedly. "My wife left me with a newborn and two other kids to raise alone. Getting through the last three years has been pure hell. But I did it, and all I wanted to do was reassure you that you can do it, too, no matter how bad it seems now."

"Who said it seems bad? I was feeling pretty good about things until you came in here."

His gaze shifted away from hers a little guiltily. All right, so she'd been deliberately hurtful. You couldn't be subtle with some people, you had to hit them over the head. Maybe the good doctor was only trying to help. Still, when Ronnie had died she'd had her fill of "helpfulness"—people with their morbid curiosity who brought over a casserole so that they could glimpse the tearful widow. The reporters, who'd somehow found out she was pregnant, wanting to do "follow-up" stories.

"You *are* angry," he said, still not the least bit

provoked. There was nothing but kindness in his voice. "I don't blame you. But I wanted you to know that if you need to talk to someone, I'm available. Maybe I can help."

"If I need to talk to someone, I have a sister and a mother and scads of family. Why would I call you?"

"Because I understand, and not too many other people do," he said as he stood and pushed the chair back where he'd found it. He paused long enough to stare at her, holding her gaze until he appeared sure he'd made his point. Then he whisked his way out of the room.

"The nerve," Millicent muttered. But she couldn't help thinking about what he'd said. Stages of grief? Sure. First you feel as if you're going to die, then you feel just wretched for a while, then you're weepy and sad but functioning again, and, she assumed, you eventually got on with your life, although she personally was still at the weepy stage.

Was she going about it all wrong?

Denial? After she was told Ronnie had died, she couldn't recall ever believing he might really be alive, that it was a mistake. She's always just accepted. That was the way she'd been raised. Her parents had lost two of their four children—one to sudden infant death syndrome, one to a senseless car accident. They'd buried parents, grandparents, aunts and uncles, cousins. They grieved for a while, then went on.

She was doing all right where Ronnie was concerned. Then again, she still had crying spells and times of doubt. But when that happened, her mother or younger sister, even her daughter, would come to the rescue, and Millicent would eventually feel better. There would always be a hole in her heart where Ronnie had been, but the pain was getting bearable.

So who was Jase Desmond to tell her she had to follow certain *steps?*

She was still fuming a few minutes later when he had the audacity to come back.

"And another thing," she began the moment he stepped into her room. But her words skidded to a halt when she saw the flowers. Jase Desmond held a basket of the most beautiful springtime blooms she'd ever seen, in every color of the rainbow. "Oh, for me?" she said inanely.

The silliest thing was, she found herself hoping that the flowers were from Jase himself, when it was more likely he'd simply picked them up from the nurse's station on his way in to torment her some more.

"For you. A peace offering. I, er, might've overstepped. I was only trying to help."

"Who says I need help?" she retorted, her ire rising again even as she appreciated the way Jase's white lab coat stretched across his broad shoulders, and that one, unruly cowlick of his shiny black hair that flopped over his forehead. As he set the flowers on the table beside her bed, she caught herself taking a deep breath, trying for a reprise of that scent she'd barely caught a whiff of when she'd first awakened to find him hovering over her.

But he didn't get close enough. He shrugged. "I can only apologize." He turned to leave.

"Wait. Please, Dr. Desmond, I'm sorry. I'm not usually such a shrew. In fact, some people say I'm a pretty nice person."

He swiveled around slowly. His gaze could've melted butter. "I guessed that."

"I'm a mass of postpartum hormones. That's my only excuse."

"You don't need any more excuses than you already have. And call me Jase."

Millicent's breath caught in her throat. Was that a slightly predatory gleam in his eye? The kind that signaled he was interested in her, male to female?

It didn't seem possible. He'd seen her in the most unflattering, undignified manner possible, and she didn't look much better now with her hair a mess and her face all pasty and puffy from lying in bed. Even if he could get past her appearance, she hadn't exactly gone out of her way to charm him. In fact, she'd done everything but drive him off with a stick.

"Jase," she said experimentally. "That's okay, I guess, since you're not really my doctor. You can call me Millicent."

"Pretty name."

"It was my great-aunt's. She was an artist. I took after her. I even look like her a little bit."

"She must have been an attractive lady."

Another uncomfortable silence, during which Millicent knew she should say something—anything—to end this flirtatious repartee. It wasn't right. Ronnie had been in his grave less than a year. She should still be wearing black, at least metaphorically. Yet here she was, responding in an undeniably sexual way to the handsome doctor's gambits.

Had to be those hormones. Funny how hormones could be blamed for all sorts of unseemly behavior.

"If that was a compliment, thank you. Now, I really need to get some rest." She looked down at the blankets, hoping he would take her at her word. Anyway, she must be mistaken about his interest. He probably flirted with every woman he met. Or maybe he was simply intrigued by her situation, her recent widowhood, which called to mind his own grief.

"I'll leave you alone, then. Oh, one other thing. Have you thought about hiring a nanny?"

Millicent laughed. What ridiculous ideas wealthy people had. "And pay her with what?"

"I happen to know an excellent nanny who would work for peanuts. She was a pediatric nurse in South Africa. I hired her to take care of my baby after my wife passed away, and she's been with me ever since."

"But if she's working for you, how could she work for me?"

"I was planning on taking a couple of weeks off to spend with the kids. Saundra—that's my nanny—

she's looking for something to keep her busy. She would love to take care of a newborn."

"Thanks, but I have my own built-in nannies— my mother, my sister, even my daughter Nancy is itching to get her hands on Mary Jane." But her mother was getting up in years. And Becky, her sister, had a job. Nancy was still in school. It *would* be nice to have a real, live nurse taking care of Mary Jane, especially since she was a preemie and not as strong a baby as Millicent's other three had been.

"Call me if you change your mind." He took a business card out of his pocket, scribbled a home number on the back, and laid it next to the flowers. "Am I being pushy again?"

That got a smile out of Millicent. "You're being kind. I appreciate your thoughtfulness."

"You know, you could call me, even if you don't want my nanny. We could pool all of our kids, and between us we'd have a baseball team. Counting the two of us."

She quickly did the math. "You have three?" Even as she said this, she realized that she hadn't immediately given him a resounding "No!" Why was that? She wouldn't call him. She couldn't even think about it.

"Ten, six, and three. All girls."

"Mine are almost ten, eight, and three. And zero, I guess. Only one boy, the eight-year-old. And no, I won't call you." The words stuck in her throat, but she managed to squeak them out. "I . . . don't date. I mean, you probably didn't mean— I don't—" she stuttered, her cheeks flushing warmly.

"Ah. I don't either, actually. At least, I haven't yet. But I intend to. I should. I mean, sometime."

Millicent had to smile. He talked a good game about not being sensitive anymore, having worked through his grief, but he was having plenty of trouble with the idea of dating again, almost as much as she was. If she had any pity in her soul, she would agree to see him, just to get him over that first hurdle. That first date.

That first betrayal.

No, she wouldn't do it. Ronnie had been the best husband, the best friend, the best father any woman could ask for. She'd had ten good years with him, packed with enough happiness to sustain her over a lifetime. It was all she needed or would ever need.

"Even if you did want to date, you wouldn't want to start with me," she said, trying to make light of the increasingly personal conversation. "You need some nice, simple girl with no problems, no baggage—no kids."

"That sounds boring."

"Nevertheless . . ."

"All right, I get the message. I'm still going to check up on you now and then until I'm sure you're back on your feet."

She should have told him not to bother. Instead she heard the words "Yes, that would be nice" coming out of her runaway mouth.

Lana Gaston, one of her dearest friends, chose that moment to pop her head in the door. Millicent felt another flush creeping up her neck as Jase's grip tightened on the clipboard he'd been holding. He smiled a greeting at Lana, but he appeared tense.

"Dr. Desmond, right?" Lana said. "You took care of my son a few months ago when the garage roof fell on him."

"I remember. The Demolition Man. He's doing all right, I hope?"

"Great, not even a scar to show for it. Um, I hear you're the one who delivered Millie's baby under less than ideal circumstances."

"It wasn't too difficult," he said with very believable modesty. "But I'm glad I was there with my catcher's mitt." He winked for Millicent's benefit, and she felt herself blushing even more hotly. "Nice to see you again, Mrs. Gaston."

As soon as the two women were alone, Lana gave Millicent a knowing look that made her want to squirm. "That's the second time I've caught him lurking close by when I came to visit you. And where did these flowers come from?"

"He's just worried, that's all. Mary Jane was the first baby he ever delivered."

"Millicent Jones, you never could lie. He's interested in you."

"No," came her hot denial. "His wife died, so we've got something in common. At least, that's what he thinks. He wanted me to talk about it."

"And did you?" Lana asked, claiming the chair Jase had abandoned.

"No. I don't talk about things like that with total strangers. The guy thinks he's a psychiatrist instead of the other kind of head doctor."

"You wouldn't talk about it with me, either," Lana reminded her. "I'm no psychiatrist, but I know it's not good to hold things inside."

"I haven't. I've talked to my mother and my sister. I think I'm doing pretty well."

Lana's stern expression softened, and she took her friend's hand. "You're doing marvelously. Anyway, I think Dr. Desmond is drop-dead gorgeous. A girl could do worse."

Millicent gasped with exaggerated melodrama. "Lana! You're almost a married woman. I hope Sloan doesn't ever hear you going on about some other guy!"

"Now, you know Sloan and I are joined at the hip these days. He's even getting into the wedding plans. But I can still appreciate a nice-looking male. And Dr. Desmond . . . wait a minute. Dr. Desmond, Dr. Desmond . . . that's ringing a bell from a very long time ago."

"He only moved to town a couple of years ago," Millicent said hastily, hoping against hope that Lana's memory wasn't that good.

But she was out of luck. Lana's face lit with the memory she'd been searching for. "Theodora! That medicine bottle she gave you. Dr. Desmond's Stomach Bitters—"

"No! Don't say it."

"But Millicent—"

"Don't say it, Lana, I mean it. Ronnie Jones is the man I married. I'm a one-man woman. There won't be any other for me, ever."

"Well, of course it's too soon now—"

"Ever!" she repeated. "Gypsy fortunetellers can be wrong."

Lana pursed her lips, then nodded. "All right, Millicent. I won't say any more about it, except you're the one who used to throw Theodora's name in Callie's and my faces. We both thought you were crazy, but it turned out you were right."

"This is different," Millicent said adamantly. She felt guilty even thinking about it. Her and Jase . . . no no no no no. Anyway, it was silly for her to think a dashing, rich doctor would look twice at a plain country girl like her. Only a fool would mistake his attention for anything more than casual, doctorly interest.

"Okay. Hey, I was just at the nursery looking in at Mary Jane. She's wiggling around more and growing!"

Millicent sighed. "I know. But she's not big enough yet. They'll release me before they do her. I don't think I can stand going home without her."

"But there aren't any problems, right?"

"No, she's perfect," Millicent said with a grin, hiding the little kernel of fear. She'd been warned that preemies often faced more health problems than full-term babies. "She'll be home and climbing the curtains in no time."

As Jase headed for home that night after evening rounds, his thoughts returned to Millicent, as they had far too frequently lately. He'd seen her several times, usually with family and friends around her. She exuded a comforting warmth and obvious love to each and every one of them. She'd been through a harrowing experience, her baby was still attached to tubes and needles, and yet her concern for her loved ones wasn't lessened because of it.

So different from Libby. His wife had loved their children to distraction, no doubt about it. But each new baby had served to insulate her further from him. She'd absorbed herself totally in her children, their happiness, their activities—and her own self-image as the perfect mother. When she socialized, it was with other young mothers while their children played together.

Jase had kept telling himself that when the children were older, when they were more independent, she would have time for him again, take more of an interest in their life together the way she had before. But seeing Millicent, he knew for certain that he'd been lying to himself. Somehow he could tell—even from the little contact he'd had with her—that frazzled mother or not, she never shut anyone out.

He couldn't count himself, because she hadn't

really let him in yet. But he was confident that would change.

As soon as he entered his house through the garage, the comforting din of children and television reached his ears. Something mysterious and exotic-smelling was cooking in the kitchen, thanks to his nanny's amazing skills. He was incredibly lucky to have found Saundra Newman, newly arrived from South Africa, newly divorced, broke, and in the E.R. after being struck by a hit-and-run driver. He'd ended up helping her attain citizenship. Before he'd known what was happening, he'd invited her to live in the apartment over his garage and take care of his children.

Sometimes things just worked out. She was a part of his family now, a grandmotherly presence even though she probably wasn't yet fifty.

"Oh, Doc Des, I'm so glad you're home," Saundra said in her precisely accented English. "That Valerie is in a horrible fit. She won't listen to a word I say."

Jase sighed. Valerie had three years till she was a teenager, but she was already acting like one. "What is it this time?"

"Some award at school. I don't know."

"Any other disasters I should be apprised of?"

"Ginger tried to eat the wallpaper again, but I stopped her. Heather's good, like always. Dinner will be ready in about five minutes."

Jase's two younger daughters barreled into the room, nearly knocking him over with their hugs of greeting. "Daddy, you better talk to Valerie," six-year-old Heather said, her voice dripping with anxiety. "She's locked herself in her room and she won't come out."

"I imagine she'll come out eventually," he said mildly, disengaging Ginger's tenacious grasp from around his leg so he could walk. He swung his youngest up in his arms, gave her a kiss on the cheek, then set her down. "You two wash up for dinner."

"But, Daddy—"

"I'll take care of Val, don't worry." He shook his head as he climbed the stairs. Heather had no memories of her mother, but she had a strong mothering instinct that made her try to fill the gap left by Libby's absence. She worried about everybody, but particularly about her moody older sister.

As he passed Valerie's room, he could hear rock music blaring from inside. Something modern and unintelligible. Rock music? At her age? He was sure that when he was ten, he'd still been interested in *Sesame Street.*

In his own room—which truly was his own, since hardly any trace of Libby remained except a couple of photographs—he changed into jeans, sweatshirt, and running shoes. Ah, that was better. On his way back toward the stairs, he tapped on Valerie's door. "Val? Dinner's ready."

"I'm not hungry," came the sullen response.

This was serious. His tall, rail-thin daughter

normally had the appetite of a sumo wrestler. "What's wrong, honey?"

The door opened a crack, then wider, a silent invitation to enter. Jase walked in, carefully stepping over discarded clothing, schoolbooks, and toys so that he could sit on the edge of the bed where his daughter had flopped down. A curtain of dark brown hair hid any glimpse of her face.

"Everything's wrong. Nobody likes me anymore."

"Why do you say that?"

"I don't just say it, I know it. Ever since Nancy Jones transferred to my class, it's all different. She's Miss Popularity. Everyone wants her to sit with them at lunch."

Nancy . . . Jones? Okay, it was a common enough name. But the little girl he'd met the night Millicent had her baby was nine years old, the right age to be in Valerie's class. "Why is it a problem that this Nancy is popular?"

"Because I'm not anymore."

Jase found this hard to believe. The phone hadn't rung any less. Valerie still got invited to sleep-overs and skating parties. "How can you tell?"

"The citizenship medal," Valerie answered, her voice muffled inside her pillow. "I was supposed to get it. Remember how I rescued the kittens in the storm drain and found homes for all of them?"

"Yes, I remember." How could he forget an episode like that? Squealing kittens all over the house, destroying the furniture and carpets.

"But then suddenly there was Nancy. She called nine-one-one when her mom was having a baby. Big deal. I mean, who *wouldn't* do that?"

Well, that answered that question. This Nancy had to be Millicent's daughter. He hadn't realized the Jones kids went to the same school that his daughters did.

"Actually, Val, it was a big deal. Remember I told you about the baby I delivered in the ambulance?"

Valerie flipped over to stare at her father. "That was the same baby?"

"Uh-huh. And Nancy Jones probably saved her mother's life by thinking quick and not panicking."

"But I didn't *have* to save those kittens. I did it because I wanted to help. Isn't that what citizenship is supposed to be?"

"Citizenship can be different things to different people. One of those things might be to accept defeat graciously and congratulate the winner."

Valerie's eyes narrowed. "What do you mean?"

"I mean that yes, you deserved to win the medal, but apparently so did Nancy. So instead of being a bad sport, you should congratulate her and be glad that you have such a glut of good citizens in your class."

"What's a glut?" she asked suspiciously.

"A lot."

"Oh. Daddy, I can't congratulate her. I don't even talk to her. I can't stand her!"

"Why's that? You're not jealous of her, are you?" Jase knew that was precisely the case. Valerie was used to being the smartest, the funniest, the most popular, and she didn't like sharing the limelight.

"No way. She's just so . . . I don't know, so perfect, I guess. She plays the viola, and everybody feels sorry for her 'cause her father died in a fire. Well, my mother died. No one feels sorry for me."

"Your mother died a long time ago, Val. Besides, you don't want pity, do you?"

"No, I guess not."

"There's always going to be people in this world you don't like, and possibly even people who don't like you. You'll do much better if you can learn now how to get along with those people. Why not invite Nancy over to play someday after school?" And maybe Jase could spend a few more innocent minutes with Nancy's mother.

Valerie looked horrified. "Forget it! She wouldn't come, anyway. She hates me."

Jase could see he wasn't going to get anywhere with this. "Well, I'm sorry you have such an enemy. Friends are much more fun. I'm going down to dinner before it gets cold. How about you?"

"Oh, all right."

"And you might think about congratulating Nancy on winning the medal. Sometimes one small gesture is all it takes to turn an enemy into a friend."

"Yeah, right, Daddy."

He'd tried. These little feuds had a way of working themselves out. Meanwhile, he wondered if his daughter had provided him with a legitimate reason to call Millicent—concerned parent to concerned parent, of course.

No, inventing excuses to see her wasn't the answer to his gridlock with Millicent. He had to accept the fact that it was too soon for her to think about him as a man, as a romantic, sexual object. He would have to bide his time, keep an eye on her, and be ready when the time came.

THREE

The bride's room at the First Methodist Church was a hotbed of nervous female energy. Lana Gaston, resplendent in her champagne-colored gown, fidgeted as one of her bridesmaids, Callie Sanger, pinned a crown of pink roses and baby's breath into her hair. Callie's mother, Wanda Calloway, was busy steaming undetectable wrinkles from the hem of Lana's dress, clucking like a nervous hen.

Meanwhile, Millicent examined herself critically in the mirror. Her raw silk dress, a soft, buttery yellow, was more snug than she would have liked.

She glanced over at Callie, at the way her identical yellow dress draped softly over her barely rounded tummy. "You know, taking the weight off after a fourth baby is a lot harder than it was the first time around. After two months I should be fitting into this size eight with no problem."

"Try fitting into a size six when you're three and

a half months pregnant," Callie said, though she sounded more proud than irritated. "Lana, if you'd planned this wedding even one week earlier or later, one of your bridesmaids would have had to let some seams out."

"Oh, hush, you two. You both look gorgeous," Lana said, pushing a spray of baby's breath off her forehead. "I couldn't wish for two prettier bridesmaids." She smiled with satisfaction. "Y'all realize this is another of Theodora's predictions come true."

"Who's Theodora?" Wanda asked through a mouthful of hairpins. She'd taken over hairdressing duties, shooing Callie away.

Lana clamped a hand over her mouth. "Oops."

Millicent smothered a laugh. Theodora was supposed to be a secret. Always.

"Just a friend who couldn't make it to the wedding," Callie answered her mother.

Sam Sanger, Callie's husband, stuck his head inside the bride's room. "Are you all about ready?"

"You bet," Lana answered without hesitation. Millicent had never seen a less nervous bride. Then again, Lana knew what she wanted this time around. She coughed a bit as Mrs. Calloway fogged her with hairspray. "Let's get this show on the road."

The wedding was small, informal, and very touching. Both of Lana's parents were deceased, so her nine-year-old son, Rob, escorted her down the aisle, then stared up at his soon-to-be stepfather with obvious adoration. The groom, Sloan Bennett, looked extra tall and handsome in his formal policeman's blues. The love between bride and groom was obvious in their eyes, their smiles, and the way they spoke their vows.

Millicent had tears streaming down her cheeks in no time—and not a tissue or handkerchief within reach. She nudged Callie, who was also sniffling. "Do you have a tissue?"

Callie shook her head.

Suddenly a handkerchief was pressed into her hand from behind. Some kind soul had seen her distress and come to the rescue. She turned to whisper her thanks, and found herself staring at Jase Desmond.

She was so surprised, all she could do was gape. What was he doing there? She hadn't seen him or talked to him in almost six weeks, since Mary Jane had been released from the hospital, though she'd often thought about him. She'd caught herself wondering if he'd started dating, and if so, what lucky woman had snagged him. He was quite a catch, she had to admit, but she wasn't fishing.

He looked even more handsome than she remembered. Sexy.

The next thing she knew, the organist was playing the recessional. By staring at Jase, she'd missed the big kiss between husband and wife. All she could do was hurry to take her place behind Callie, on the arm of her assigned groomsman, and let herself be whisked up the aisle in a daze.

The vestibule was a melee of hugging and kissing. Millicent pushed Jase from her thoughts long enough to wish the bride and groom continued happiness. But when the small crowd moved en masse to the church hall for the reception, she spotted Jase again—with a gorgeous redhead clinging to his arm—and she found herself short of breath. He looked extremely civilized in his light gray suit, but there was a vein of restless energy there too.

Later she spotted him on the dance floor with his date, doing an easy two-step to a George Jones song. They talked and laughed easily, but he wasn't holding her very close, Millicent noticed. Then she chided herself for taking pleasure in the fact.

"Millie? You okay?" Callie asked. "Here, have a piece of cake." She thrust a plate heaped with white cake and frosting at Millicent.

"Ah, no thanks. The dress is tight enough as it is."

"Okay, I'll eat it. This eating for two is fun."

"Do you know why Jase Desmond was invited to the wedding?" Millicent blurted out.

"Who?"

"That guy over there with the redhead. Don't stare!" She'd die if Jase knew she'd taken such an unseemly interest in him.

"It's hard not to stare. He's a hunk if I ever saw one. Who is he?"

"The doctor who delivered my baby. He also treated Lana's son in the E.R. a few months ago, but I didn't think he and Lana knew each other well."

Callie studied the couple with interest. Then she snapped her fingers. "I've got it. It's the red-head who was invited. Her name's Robin something. She was Lana's roommate at Stockton. The doc is probably her date."

"Oh, that would make sense." Millicent felt relieved, then a little let down. She'd been harboring a silly fantasy that maybe he'd come to the wedding because of her somehow.

"Mom. Mom?"

Millicent turned to find Nancy pulling urgently at her sleeve. "You won't believe who's here. Dr. Desmond. And you know what I found out? He's Valerie Desmond's dad."

"Valerie . . . oh, her?" The one who'd gotten upset with Nancy over the citizenship medal. Millicent let this new piece of information sink in. Through Nancy's animated descriptions, Millicent had come to think of Valerie as a jealous, ill-mannered snip. And she was Jase's daughter? Didn't seem possible that a man like Jase would have anything but gorgeous, polite children.

"Omigosh, he's coming over here," Nancy said, searching for a means of escape.

Omigosh indeed. Millicent grabbed her daughter by the ponytail to prevent her panicked flight. "Stay here and show some manners, please." She would just as soon not face him alone when she was feeling so flustered. Nancy made a good buffer. And thank goodness Jase was with a date. That made him a little bit safer territory, although at the moment the redhead was nowhere in evidence.

"Do you think he knows? About the medal?" Nancy asked urgently.

"Oh, probably not," Millicent said. Not unless his daughter blabbed about it endlessly the way Nancy had.

He approached boldly, resolutely, then squeezed her hand lightly in greeting. "Hello, Millicent." His deep voice gave her a pleasurable chill, while his innocent touch warmed her to the core. "I thought I might find you here at this wedding. How's Mary Jane?"

Millicent couldn't help but glow at the mention of her newest daughter. "Thriving. Eating like a horse. You wouldn't recognize her. I would have brought her here, but you know how babies can spoil weddings by crying. My sister is keeping her and Lily for the day."

"That's great." His smile was warm, approving. "Hi, Nancy."

"Hi, Dr. Desmond," Nancy said in a small voice.

"I've heard a lot about you in the past few weeks."

"Mmm?" Nancy looked like a deer caught by headlights.

He smiled. "My daughter Valerie is in your class. She's told me about you. Something about a citizenship medal?" He gave her a teasing wink.

"I didn't deserve it," Nancy said miserably, the words rushing to get out as she literally wrung her hands. "Valerie saved those kittens. I voted for her to win. Um, 'scuse me, I need some punch." She fled.

"Oops. I think," Jase said, "that I just made your daughter very uncomfortable. I only meant to tease her. Sorry."

"In case you hadn't heard about it, there's some rivalry going on between our two daughters."

"Rivalry? How about World War Three? I told Valerie she was being a bad sport about the medal and that she should congratulate Nancy. She won't do it."

"Nancy hasn't exactly been Miss Congeniality. She gloated about that medal for an hour when she got home. But I guess I should explain. Nancy transferred into the accelerated class just this semester. She's had some trouble fitting in. She's shy, like I am, and bookish, and she plays the viola, which some of the kids make fun of. To have her classmates vote to give her an award—that was really important to her. Not that that's any excuse for being rude."

"You're shy?" Jase deftly maneuvered her to one of the tables and pulled out a chair for her. "I wouldn't say so. You have no trouble talking to me."

Now, how had he shifted the conversation to her? "I am shy, trust me," she said, taking the chair. "I never had a date in high school. I barely talked to anyone. Speaking of dates, I guess you've managed to cross that hurdle. Congratulations." She tried to sound sincere. "Um, where did she go?" Millicent raised her eyebrows just a tad, letting him know that if he intended to flirt, he'd better think twice.

"She went to find the rest room. And she's not really my date. She's a nurse I work with. I overheard her mention she was going to this wedding, and how she didn't want to go alone, so—"

"So you did the chivalrous thing? Sounds like a date to me."

"Chivalrous? I groveled until she agreed to bring me with her."

Millicent stared. Surely this man never had to ask twice. "Why?"

"I knew you'd be here."

Her mouth went dry. "I thought . . . I mean . . . oh, dear, I think I've had too much champagne." She looked everywhere but at him.

"Are you okay? Should I get you some water?" He was only compounding her dizziness by sitting so close to her. Way too close. His scent, clean and masculine, teased her like some exotic intoxicant more potent than champagne.

"No, I'll be fine, really." Might as well take the bull by the horns. She worked up her courage and looked directly into his changeable hazel eyes, which right now looked almost gold, like a lion's. "Why did you want to see me?"

He flashed a guilty smile. "Let's just call it overwhelming curiosity. We went through something together, you and I. It's not an experience I can easily dismiss. I couldn't resist a chance to check up on you the way I promised I would, see how you and your brood are doing."

A perfectly innocent explanation. Millicent chided herself for thinking his interest was any more personal. He found her an interesting case, an object of fascination. That was all. Thank goodness.

His next words propelled her out of the comfort zone she'd been trying to settle into. "Look, I know you're not ready to date. But someday you will be. And I'd like to be around when that happens."

Millicent was flattered . . . excited . . . *incredulous* . . . then quickly deflated. "I won't ever date again, Jase."

"I felt that way too."

She knew he was only trying to comfort. But his attitude was like a red flag in her face. "And you think I'll 'come out of it'?"

"Of course you will."

"And do you suppose that every person deals with a spouse's death in exactly the same way? That I should feel and react a certain way because that's the way you did it?"

"Grief does follow a certain pattern, though it's not exactly the same with everyone."

Millicent folded her arms defensively. "Well, I'm not following any pattern. Ronnie was my husband, the father of my children. There won't ever be anyone else for me." Her words were a challenge.

His voice was low, seductive. "Who are you trying to convince, me or yourself?"

She struggled for a stinging comeback. Struggled and failed. He was right. She found Jase Desmond attractive. Even now her body betrayed her by reacting to him. She could feel her nipples puckering, her stomach tightening, and heat building somewhere deep inside.

His offer, his implied invitation, was tempting. Or at least it would be at some point in the future, if he persisted. And that realization disturbed her profoundly. She did not want the messiness of another relationship, especially with a man who had his own baggage and a houseful of motherless kids.

Her priority was her own children.

She was afraid he would demand an answer from her. Instead he switched tacks. "I'm not asking you to have an affair with me," he said softly. "I'm looking for companionship. Something besides the treadmill of work and kids, work and kids. I want to rejoin the land of the living. We could be good for each other."

"So, you're saying we'd just be friends?" Millicent grabbed onto that concept with both hands. She must have misunderstood before. He didn't really want to date. He just needed another adult his age to talk to. Maybe the redheaded nurse was a poor conversationalist.

"Sure, for now."

She sat up straighter. "Not 'for now.' Forever. That part won't change."

He gave her an appraising look. "Fine."

She was not convinced he believed her. Worse, she wasn't sure she believed herself. She was a grieving widow with a new baby. She shouldn't be having this confusion. The choice should be so simple—cut this man off at the knees.

But she couldn't find the words.

The redhead reappeared, all smiles. "I've never seen Lana looking so happy. She certainly didn't glow like that when she married her first husband." The woman held out her hand to Millicent. "Hi, I'm Robin Milhaus."

"Millicent Jones," Millicent said, immediately liking the woman despite not wanting to. Her handshake was firm and friendly.

"Oh, of course! I took care of your baby at the hospital. I'm a pediatric nurse." Robin turned to Jase. "I ran into a couple of old college friends. We're heading out to the lake as soon as this gig winds down—there's some kind of concert going on. Want to come with us?" She turned to Millicent. "You're welcome to come too. The more the merrier."

"Oh, I couldn't," Millicent said immediately. "I have my kids with me."

"That's perfect! Some of the other people are bringing kids too. It's a family-type outing."

Jase looked at Millicent expectantly. "What do you say? We could go for an hour or two."

Wait a minute. Why did it seem like suddenly *she* was Jase's date, instead of Robin?

"Hey, I've got an even better plan," Jase said, warming to the idea. "I'll pick up my girls and Saundra, their nanny. You can pick up your other two and your sister, and we'll make a day of it."

"C'mon, Millicent. It'll be fun," Robin said. "Besides, I want to see Mary Jane again. She's a doll."

Okay, so she had a soft spot when it came to anyone fussing over Mary Jane. Robin had even remembered the baby's name. Now Millicent was having a hard time turning down Robin's invitation. "Uh . . ." How could she get out of this?

"Mom!" Nancy provided a welcome interruption. She cast a nervous, not altogether friendly look at Jase. "Come on. The bride and groom are getting ready to leave!"

Millicent found herself swept up in the crowd of well-wishers bidding the happy couple good-bye. Someone thrust a packet of rice into her hand. She hurriedly threw it, missing her target by a mile.

Lana and Sloan waved their good-byes as they headed for their silver limousine, which would take them to the airport. At the last moment Lana carelessly tossed her bridal bouquet over her shoulder.

As Millicent watched the bundle of pink roses arc through the air, she could only stand in dumbfounded wonder. It was as if an unseen hand were guiding the flowers like a missile—straight into her arms.

Everyone around her grew silent, obviously uncomfortable as they stared at her clutching the flowers.

"Mom," Nancy whispered, frowning with disapproval.

Millicent thrust the flowers at the nearest person, who happened to be Robin. "Here. I don't think this was meant for me."

Robin smiled sympathetically. "Sure, I'll take it." She held the bouquet aloft. "Any single millionaires out there want to propose?" Her joke produced a ripple of laughter, ending the awkward moment.

Jase saw the whole spectacle, and now he shook his head. Of all people to catch the bouquet—a woman who'd just declared she would never date again, much less marry. He went to her, though he resisted the urge to touch her. His touch wasn't what she needed right now.

"Looks like things are winding down. So how about the lake? Robin said there are a bunch of different bands playing at the band shell all day—some country, some bluegrass, a little gospel."

"I don't know, Jase . . ."

"It's just a group of people—friends—getting together. It's not a date."

She felt trapped. To refuse would make her look like a recluse, a person who wasn't dealing with life. And she *was* handling her life just fine, despite Jase's concerns. "Well, all right. I'm sure the kids will enjoy it. Seems like I haven't taken them anywhere for ages."

"The kids will enjoy what?" asked Nancy, who had suddenly reappeared at her mother's elbow.

"We're all going out to the lake for a concert at the band shell," Millicent announced, thinking Nancy would be thrilled.

Nancy's eyes widened. "All *who?*"

"Well, whoever wants to go. Dr. Desmond is going, and his friend Robin, and some other people. There's going to be a bunch of kids there."

Nancy stood on her tiptoes and whispered in Millicent's ear. "Dr. Desmond's kids? That means Valerie!"

"Yes, it does," Millicent said firmly. She'd momentarily forgotten about the feud between Nancy and Jase's daughter, but this seemed like a good opportunity to get the girls together on neutral ground and suggest a peace treaty.

"I'm not going," Nancy declared.

Millicent, appalled by her daughter's rudeness, grew all the more determined to force the issue. "We'll talk about it in the car. Go find your brother and meet me at the van."

After Nancy had flounced off, Jase gave Millicent a sympathetic look.

"I apologize," she said. "Nancy will apologize, too, if I have anything to say about it."

Jase shrugged. "Forget it. Valerie won't be any more pleased. But maybe we can get them to talk."

"Exactly what I was thinking. I figured the feud would blow over, but it hasn't. It's time we dealt with it." It was also time to deal with her annoying attraction to Jase. She was probably just going through a phase, a reaction to the loneliness that had clawed at her recently. Having a new baby and no father with whom to share the joy and fears brought home her loss in a hundred different ways, every day.

So, she would spend time with Jase, see that he was just an ordinary man like any other, and get over it.

Destiny Park was a small oasis of wooded hills and meadows surrounding Destiny Lake. The city's forefathers had lacked a little imagination when naming things, Jase thought. But they'd created a nice park, with a band shell, an old-fashioned carousel, and plenty of picnic areas.

Right now the park was packed with families, college kids from nearby Stockton University, and roving bands of adolescents. Robin and her group of fun-loving college friends fit right in, but Jase felt apart from it all, as if something were missing.

Or someone. Millicent hadn't showed yet.

He'd agreed to meet her at the lake, at a place called Flagpole Hill, in an hour's time. She was almost fifteen minutes late.

Maybe this hadn't been such a good idea. He'd taken the coward's way out by not informing Valerie of Nancy Jones's impending arrival, so he had that little unpleasantry to look forward to. Aside from that, he was worried that he'd pushed Millicent too hard. After all, her husband had died less than a year ago.

Then again, he wished someone had pushed him sooner after Libby's death. He'd wallowed in his grief for too long, immersing himself in work and children, existing from day to day instead of living. He hated to think of delicate Millicent experiencing that kind of pain.

When at last he saw her, trudging up the hill with a stroller and a parade of children, his heart lifted and the sun came out from behind the clouds. She hadn't stood him up after all.

He waved to her. She waved back, tentatively, he thought. Probably having second thoughts. Maybe he should be too. He was dreadfully out of practice with this man-woman stuff. Other than a couple of one-night stands—something he wasn't proud of—there hadn't been anyone since Libby.

Not that he hadn't had plenty of opportunities in recent months to get back into the swing. He wasn't naive. A widowed doctor—even one with a ready-made family—was attractive to some women regardless of his looks or personality. But he hadn't really been tempted until now. Until Millicent.

He met the Jones clan halfway up Flagpole Hill. The two older children greeted him with cool, formal handshakes.

"I'm sorry if I was rude earlier, Dr. Desmond," Nancy said in what was obviously a scripted speech. "It was nice of you to invite us along." She practically choked on the words, earning a frown from her mother.

"I'm glad you could make it," Jase said, flashing Millicent his warmest smile. She'd changed from that yellow silk number into pink shorts and a striped top that made her look more like a teenager than the mother of four. He grabbed an ice chest from her, and a bag of groceries from Becky, Millicent's younger sister.

Becky was her older sister's antithesis. Tall, thickset, blond, and bosomy, she was nonetheless charming in her own, blustery way.

"Can't take this bunch anywhere without lots of provisions," Becky said. "You're a lifesaver."

"No problem. Our group has some territory staked out under those trees. Follow me." He led the parade to a patchwork of blankets and quilts laid out on the grass beneath two huge cottonwood trees. Robin and her friends were busy grilling hamburgers on a hibachi. A group of toddlers, one his own Ginger, were crawling around on the blankets or dozing under Saundra's watchful eye. The older kids were nearby playing a spirited game of Frisbee. They were surrounded by families and couples of every description doing similar things while the music of a bluegrass band drifted lazily on the breeze.

The scene would have been idyllic if not for the tension radiating from Millicent. Her discomfiture was evident in every move she made, even in the way she laid out her own blankets slightly apart from the others.

She immediately immersed herself in fussing with Mary Jane.

Jase knelt down beside them, determined to make her feel more at ease. "My, she *has* grown. Can I hold her?"

"Of course." As always, Millicent beamed at the subject of her new daughter. "Her pediatrician thinks she might be having some developmental problems, but I don't see it. She's lifting her head already."

Alarm bells went off in Jase's brain. Developmental problems? Mary Jane's pediatrician was Nora Daas, one of the best. If Nora thought there was a problem . . .

Instinctively Jase shied away from the possibility. Preemies often did show developmental quirks, but they usually resolved themselves with no permanent repercussions. Nora was probably just issuing the standard precautionary statements to Millicent.

Just the same, he found himself studying the child. Was it only his imagination, or did Mary Jane's left eye wander a bit? He surreptitiously checked the baby's grip. She could grab on hard with her right hand, but her left-hand grasp was negligible. And when she wiggled and squirmed on the blanket, was there something . . . out of balance about the way she moved?

No. It was simply paranoia on his part. He dealt

with sick babies on a regular basis, and Mary Jane wasn't sick. She was perfect. Millicent could not have given birth to a child with any sort of defect. She had been dealt enough hardship for one life. Fate could not be that cruel.

FOUR

Millicent found herself enjoying the concert despite her misgivings. The two toddlers, Ginger and Lily, had formed an instant camaraderie and were now sitting on a blanket together, happily throwing grapes at each other. Will, who was so easygoing that he could get along with anyone under any circumstances, had joined in the Frisbee game with some of the other children.

Mary Jane was passed from one pair of eager arms to the next, eating up the attention with a spoon. Millicent's sister, Becky, was flirting with one of Robin's friends. Only her and Jase's oldest daughters seemed unhappy. Sulky Nancy had climbed up into one of the cottonwood trees with a book, and Valerie had flopped down on a far corner of the blankets with a Walkman, closing herself off from everyone.

"Those two girls have more in common than

they think," Jase whispered in Millicent's ear. His breath was warm, ruffling her hair. She felt a silly urge to lean closer, to actually bring his lips in contact with her when he spoke again. "I can't believe they're both so stubborn."

"I can," Millicent said. "About Nancy, anyway. She's like me in some ways, but she's much more strong willed than I ever was."

"Now, why do you think you're not strong willed? You would have to be, to manage four kids the way you do. And you certainly haven't taken any guff from me."

He'd done it again, turned the conversation to her. She didn't like talking about herself. There were so many more interesting subjects in the world. "I do what I have to do to survive," she said simply.

Jase stretched his long, tanned legs out beside hers. He'd changed from his suit into faded cutoff jeans that molded to his anatomy with disconcerting familiarity. He was so close that his upper arm brushed against her sleeve. Even that slight contact made her blood surge. It was so inappropriate for her to feel this way, yet she couldn't deny it. Damn Theodora, anyway! If not for the fortuneteller and her infernal predictions, Millicent was sure this wouldn't be happening to her.

"I want to do more than survive," Jase said.

"Sometimes that's all one can manage."

"I want to live again."

"This *is* living," she argued. "It's a beautiful

evening, the music's great, we had a delicious picnic, we're surrounded by our children. What could be better?" She was all too afraid she knew the answer to that question, at least the answer Jase was contemplating.

"This is a start," he said. "But I think we *can* do better. Eventually." The suggestion in his tone was unmistakable.

Millicent kept trying to convince herself that Jase was motivated by kindness, by curiosity, by the challenge she represented—by anything but genuine desire. And then he went and said something so outrageously provocative that she was forced to admit she was deluding herself.

The man wanted her. Waves of sexuality poured off of him, engulfing her. She was drowning in it. It couldn't be her imagination this time.

She scrambled to her feet. "I'm going for a walk," she announced abruptly.

"I'll come with you. I'm getting a little restless myself."

Naturally. She knew she should tell him to bug off, that she needed some time alone. But to say that would be admitting her reaction to him, and she couldn't risk letting him know how he affected her. That would be her secret, and she would carry it to her grave. She couldn't help her hormonal agitation, but she could control her actions. She at least had that.

A young man was riding a horse at the far end of the park, showing off for a group of female admirers. Millicent headed that way. Jase walked beside her looking graceful, relaxed, while she was a bundle of nerves.

Some bales of hay had been set out for impromptu seating. Millicent found an empty corner of one and sat down next to an old man. There was another space on the next bale for Jase. But the old man promptly departed, and Jase claimed his seat. Did he have to sit so close?

"I love horses," she said, hoping to keep the conversation to a safe, neutral topic. "I had a pony when I was a little girl. I've been thinking about buying the kids a horse."

"I understand they're a lot of trouble," Jase pointed out. "And money."

"I've got the money—some, anyway. Ronnie's life insurance. We agreed that if anything ever happened to either one of us . . ." Her voice caught. *Way to go, Millie. Nice and neutral.* She continued resolutely. ". . . the other would use that money for the kids. So Nancy has her viola lessons. And Will, I think, would be interested in learning to ride."

Jase obviously hadn't missed the thickness in her throat, or the shine of tears that undoubtedly graced her eyes. What was wrong with her? She hadn't cried in front of anyone in months. He looked at her with an understanding that took her breath away.

He'd been right about one thing, she supposed. He understood, better than most people. She smiled, acknowledging his sympathy, letting him know she was all right. It turned out to be a nice moment.

Until he spoke again.

"Have you attended any grief counseling, or a support group?"

Millicent felt herself prickling up like a porcupine. "Spilling my guts to strangers? No, thanks. I already told you, I have built-in counselors." Whom she hadn't confided in for a long time. She was beginning to feel as if she'd burdened her family enough with her troubles.

"I attended a group. It helps a lot. Yeah, the people are strangers, but that made it easier for me. Whatever was said, no matter how embarrassing, you knew you probably wouldn't see those people again outside the group."

Millicent sprang to her feet, arms crossed tightly over her breasts. "Why are you doing this?"

He appeared puzzled as he slowly rose to his feet, too, towering over her. Looking way too strong and masculine. "Doing what?"

"Throwing my grief in my face all the time. Reminding me of it."

"I don't have to remind you of it," he said softly. "It's there, surrounding you like a cloud. It's with you constantly. You have a hard time getting through a conversation without getting misty."

"So? That's normal, I think. It hasn't even been a year." She stalked off. He followed.

"I'm not saying you're abnormal, Millicent," he

said to the back of her head. "You're going through a painful time. I'm trying to help you—from the perspective of someone who's been there."

She halted and whirled around so fast, he almost plowed right into her. "Why? No, don't answer that."

"Why not? Are you afraid of the answer?"

"No! I'm not afraid of anything." Her denial sounded impossibly juvenile, defensive, and utterly unbelievable. She was scared to death, and he knew it.

"If it helps, I'm afraid too," he said, his voice almost a caress itself. He brushed a strand of her hair behind her ear. The gesture was achingly gentle, but not as innocent as it might seem to a casual onlooker. "I guess it's like falling off a horse."

She shook her head in denial. "That's an idiotic comparison."

"Is it? The longer I wait, the harder it gets."

That did it. So, she was his testing ground? Forget kindness, or challenge, or all those other motives she'd assigned to him for his interest in her. She was a hurdle to be cleared.

"You're so damn eager to get back in the race? Fine. I'll give you a leg up." The distance between them was only a few inches, anyway. She grasped his shoulders, squeezed her eyes shut, and clamped her lips on his.

He was frozen at first, with pure shock, she imagined. But that didn't last long. Within a split second he responded with instinctual heat. His mouth moved, taking command. What had started as a lesson to be taught turned quickly into something Millicent hadn't bargained for.

For a few seconds she let her own instincts conquer everything else. She opened her mouth against his, tasting him, reveling in the fire and the smoky heat of their mingled desire. The last rays of the dying sun peeked through the trees, spotlighting their moment of passion.

Then, as if she'd been doused with ice water, Millicent came to her senses. She broke the kiss, pushed herself away, and stood staring at him and gasping. What had she done? Had she gone crazy?

It was obvious that Jase was not unmoved. He raked an unsteady hand through his dark hair. "Just what, exactly, was that supposed to prove?"

Why had she done it? God help her, she knew the answer. She'd *wanted* to kiss him, and obviously her sneaky subconscious had been looking for an excuse, no matter how feeble, to do it.

Now she had to bluff her way through this, to somehow erase the idiocy of the past few moments, or to at least discount it. "It proves that nothing has changed." She was such a liar! Everything had changed. "Do you feel any better? I sure don't." That, at least, was the truth.

"I feel a lot of things," he said. " 'Better' probably isn't the best way to describe it. I'm relieved we got that first kiss out of the way. But I'm disappointed that it was born out of anger, no matter how much I enjoyed it."

"First, last, and only kiss," she ground out. "You said you didn't want an affair, remember?"

"I said I wouldn't ask you for that. Big difference. Anyway, you're the one who started the kissing."

Damn, he was right. Maybe she'd thought that by kissing him, she could satisfy her curiosity and get it out of her system, or some such nonsense. If that had been her aim, she'd failed miserably. Her body was still thrumming from the aftereffects of the kiss. If anything, she'd thrown fuel on the fire. "It's too soon," she said miserably.

Jase sighed. "Thank God."

"What?"

"If it's too soon now, that means you're seeing some point in the future when the time will be right. You've never admitted that before."

Funny, she didn't recall admitting anything. "I think your optimism is a little unfounded. I've told you before, and I'll tell you again, that I have no intention of becoming involved with another man—ever."

"The road to hell is paved with—"

"Oh, don't say it. You're impossible." It would be so much easier if he would just get angry at her, instead of accepting her horrid behavior with such smug approval. "It's late. I should be getting home." She stalked away, feeling his presence behind her, half hoping he would say something to make her stay. Or at least something that would make her feel okay about what she'd done.

But he remained silent.

Rounding up the kids and packing up was another ordeal. Lily was sound asleep, Mary Jane was cranky from having her routine upset, and Will objected strenuously to giving up play with his new-found friends. Only Nancy was impatient to be gone.

Somehow, drawing on her organizational skills and the edge of panic Jase had given her, she gathered everything up. Jase offered to walk her to her car, but she coolly refused. She thanked Robin for including the Jones family in her festivities, then made her escape.

She didn't relax until her car was on the road and heading for home. Then she tensed again as she remembered another problem that had to be dealt with.

"Nancy," she began, "I'm very disappointed in you."

"Mom, I don't like her," Nancy retorted hotly, close to tears. "I think I'm old enough to pick my own friends."

Millicent's patience was wearing thin. "I'm not saying you have to be best friends with Valerie. But to completely ignore her, not to mention everyone else, was downright rude. I've taught you better than that. You have to be polite to everyone, even people you don't like."

"It wasn't like *she* tried to be nice. She was zoned out all afternoon on that stupid rock music she likes."

"I'll agree, her behavior was no better than yours."

There was a long pause. When Nancy spoke again, there was a sly, accusing note to her voice. "Anyway, who are you to talk about *behavior?*"

Millicent said nothing. Ordinarily she wouldn't have let such cheeky back talk stand unchallenged. But Nancy's vague accusation had sent a chill down her spine. What had her daughter seen, or sensed, between her and Jase?

She glanced over at Becky in the passenger seat, but apparently her sister hadn't been paying much attention to the conversation, or she would have jumped on Nancy's provocative question. Thank goodness.

Later, when Becky had gone home, the house was quiet, and the younger children were asleep, Millicent called Nancy out of her room and into the kitchen. This was where they often had their more intimate conversations—about Ronnie, about growing up, about life in general.

"You want some hot chocolate?"

"It's too hot for hot chocolate," Nancy said warily.

"How about cold chocolate milk, then?"

"Yeah, okay."

Millicent busied herself with squirting chocolate syrup into two tall glasses of milk while she composed her next words. She didn't even want to have this conversation, but she had to. "Nancy," she finally said, "what did you mean when you questioned my behavior?"

"You know."

She was afraid she did. "Spell it out for me."

"You and Dr. Desmond. Mom, how could you carry on like that when you're barely even widowed?"

Millicent smiled briefly at the notion that her and Jase's behavior could be termed "carrying on." But her daughter's anguish was too real for her to be amused for long. "It's been almost a year since your father died. During that time, I've practically buried myself out here in the country with you kids. Not that you aren't a great comfort to me, but sometimes I need to spend time with other adults."

"You kissed him!" Nancy accused. Her chocolate milk sat untouched. "I was up in the tree. I saw you."

Oddly enough, Millicent found herself wanting to defend her behavior, even though a couple of hours earlier she'd condemned herself a hundred different ways. "I'm sorry," was all she could think of to say. She sat down and sipped at her own milk, trying to cool her throat. She hated her urge to cry.

"Did you just forget about Dad?"

"Maybe for one brief moment, I did," she murmured, more to herself than her daughter. How could she have done that? Ronnie had been her whole life. "Sometimes, when someone dies, there's a big, aching hole that begs to be filled. And sometimes the people left behind try to fill that hole any way they can, even if it's the wrong way."

"I don't want you to see him anymore," Nancy said belligerently.

Millicent hid a sad smile. Her daughter sounded for all the world like a parent scolding a wayward teenager. It was on the tip of her tongue to assure Nancy that she had no intention of seeing Dr. Desmond ever again—that she would never betray Ronnie's memory. But the words wouldn't come. It was easier to make the promise to herself than to Nancy. She wondered why.

Was it because she feared breaking the promise?

"I have no plans to see Dr. Desmond again," she said. "But, as I've discovered, what gets planned and what happens are sometimes two different things. Dr. Desmond is lonely. His wife died. He seems to think I can make him feel better. And it's awfully hard to turn him away."

"So you kissed him out of pity?" Nancy's voice dripped with skepticism.

"No. That was an impulse, one I regret." Because the time wasn't right. "I certainly don't pity him. It's just . . ." Oh, how could she explain it when she didn't understand what was happening herself? Nancy was an insightful little girl, but a nine-year-old couldn't possibly comprehend the raw needs that sometimes drove adults.

She put her arm around Nancy's shoulders. "I can't make any promises about the future, except one: You, and your brother and sisters, will always come first. I'll never do anything to hurt you."

Nancy abruptly picked up her glass and drained it with a series of noisy gulps. She wiped her mouth with the back of her hand, then looked at Millicent with hooded eyes. "Okay, Mom. I'm going to bed now."

"All right." As mother-daughter talks went, this one hadn't been a crashing success, but it would have to do for now. "Have sweet dreams."

Nancy got up, started for the door, then turned and quickly pecked Millicent on the cheek before fleeing.

The Desmond household was finally quiet. Jase took a quick shower, then climbed into his king-size bed, which had been looking larger and emptier to him lately.

After Millicent's departure one of Robin's friends had flirted unmercifully with him. She'd been pretty enough, and a few weeks earlier he might have welcomed her company. But she'd only succeeded in irritating him. He wasn't interested in some shallow young woman who'd done nothing in her life but attend college and party. She might have filled his bed, but what would they talk about?

Before turning off the bedside lamp, he picked up a brass-framed photograph from the nightstand. The picture was an old one of Libby with Valerie and Heather, when Heather was still in diapers. He had no pictures of his wife alone.

"Well, Libby, what do you think of your old man now?" he asked aloud. "I kissed Millicent Jones."

The photo stared blankly back at him with a frozen, eternal smile.

"Actually, she kissed me, but I certainly didn't object." He'd been shocked clear down to his toes—then incredibly turned on. He'd almost forgotten how good a feeling that was, and how miserable it felt to have such potent desire unfulfilled. His mind was filled with visions of Millicent, soft and pliant beneath him, their limbs tangled in damp sheets. He remembered, over and over, the texture of her hair where he'd touched it so briefly, the feel of her lips that hinted of a rich well of passion beneath her ladylike demeanor.

He flipped the photograph face-down, then suddenly shoved it into the nightstand drawer. He didn't think it was wrong for him to have fantasies about Millicent, but it felt wrong to do it while staring at a picture of his wife! He ought to have more respect for Libby's memory.

Jase slept restlessly, which made his twelve-hour shift in the emergency room the next day a trial to be endured, even after consuming a gallon of coffee. But there was no possibility of begging off. The hospital was short-staffed, and every doctor had to do his or her stint in the E.R. His regular patient load was pretty heavy right now, too, for which he was grateful. Between that and the extra shifts, he had little time to dwell on his dilemma with Millicent.

She needed time. He knew that. He was prepared to give it to her—at least another month. Keeping busy would make the time pass more quickly, he figured. Then he would test the waters again, although he couldn't imagine what ruse he could dream up next time to run into her. It was unlikely they would keep showing up at the same weddings. He didn't want to call her up. Frontal attacks had failed miserably with her. The situation called for subtlety.

As it turned out, he didn't need to manufacture any excuses to see her, and he didn't have to wait a month. On Thursday, less than a week later, he received an urgent page.

"The principal at Valerie's school wants you to come up there right away," the operator informed him.

"Why? She's not sick, is she? Hurt?"

"No, nothing like that. Mr. Reynolds said it was a, um, disciplinary problem."

Requiring his instant presence? That was odd, Jase thought as he hung his lab coat in his locker. Valerie had never gotten into trouble before. What could it possibly be? She was only ten. Well, no use fearing the worst. He would know soon enough.

The answer became abundantly clear the moment he was ushered into the principal's office at Henry Brown Middle School. There sat his daughter, head bowed, in a metal chair. The white sailor's blouse and navy blue jeans she'd worn as she left for school that morning were now smeared with a rainbow of colors and textures. Her hair, which Saundra had meticulously braided, was hanging loose and grimy, smeared with something that looked decidedly like cherry Jell-O.

In another chair on the opposite side of the office sat another little girl, looking equally disheveled. It was hard to tell what color her clothes had once been, and her light brown hair was mixed with what looked like strands of spaghetti. She was none other than Nancy Jones.

Before Jase could find his voice, the office door opened again and Millicent burst through, with Mary Jane and Lily in tow. "What happened?" she demanded, her gaze landing first on Jase, then on Mr. Reynolds, then on Nancy. "Honey, are you all right?"

"It was a food fight," Reynolds said tightly. "Neither girl would give me an explanation. But I understand there was some foul language involved."

For a few more moments all Jase could do was stare, dumbfounded, at his disgraced daughter. A sideways glance at Millicent told him she was just as shocked. She set Mary Jane's infant seat onto the floor, then plopped a nodding Lily onto a chair. For the first time, Jase noticed that Millicent was less than pristine herself. Her denim shorts and T-shirt were covered with red-orange stains, and even her face bore smudges of the same hue.

She knelt down in front of Nancy. "You want to tell me what this is about?"

"No."

"Well, you'd better, or you're going to be stuck in the principal's office for a long time. 'Cause we're not leaving until this is settled."

Nancy looked up, her face tear-streaked. "All right. All right, I'll tell you." She pointed an accusing finger at Valerie. "She said you were a slut."

Valerie was immediately out of her chair, pointing too. "Daddy, *she* said she saw you *kissing* her mother. And all I said was, 'If that's true, than your mother must be . . .'" She cast an uneasy glance at Millicent. "Because you wouldn't do that."

Millicent blushed several shades of pink, and Jase could have cheerfully throttled his daughter. Mr. Reynolds didn't look very comfortable himself.

"Could we have a few minutes alone with them?" Jase asked the principal.

"Certainly." He skedaddled out of the room faster than a rat deserting a sinking ship.

Jase had no trouble finding the right words. "Look at me, Valerie."

She looked up, a mutinous expression on her face.

"The fact of the matter is, your mother is gone, and she's not coming back. Nancy's father is gone too. And if Mrs. Jones and I want to . . . kiss, there's nothing wrong with that."

"I know, I guess," Valerie admitted. "I was just trying to get at Nancy. I didn't mean anything personal against you, Mrs. Jones. I'm sorry."

"Apology accepted," Millicent said with admirable grace. "Nancy, what else do you have to say?"

"I wasn't trying to pick a fight," she explained. "I told Valerie about the kiss because I wanted her to . . . to keep her father away from you." She glanced nervously at Jase. "You're very nice and all, Dr. Desmond. But my mom doesn't want another husband. You're just confusing her."

"How do you know what your mother wants?" Valerie piped in.

"Because she *told* me," Nancy shot back.

"Hold it right there," Millicent broke in. "In the first place, no one has said anything about a new husband for me. But you should know, Nancy, that some of the things we've said over the past year were said in the middle of pain and grieving for your father. For instance, you once said you would visit his grave every day. But I haven't held you to that."

"Yeah, and you said you would never make another coconut cream pie because it was Dad's favorite, but Will bugged you into making one last week."

"Exactly."

"So, you're saying you might get married again someday?"

"I don't know, Nancy. I really don't think so. But as time passes, I'm finding I do feel differently about some things. I used to think I would never go out in public again, but I've done that, and I've even enjoyed myself."

"I'll say."

Millicent stiffened. Whatever understanding she'd been cultivating with her daughter seemed to evaporate. "Listen to me, young lady. If I want to see Dr. Desmond, I will. And if I want to kiss him, I will. We're both adults, we're both free, and I don't need my nine-year-old daughter to be my conscience. Is that understood?"

"Yes, ma'am," Nancy said, not very convincingly.

Jase didn't know who was more surprised by her declaration, him or Millicent herself. He suspected all the talk about dating and kissing was more to make a point, not a statement of her plans for the future. But it delighted him nonetheless.

"As for this ridiculous feud between you and Valerie, it's going to end right here and now."

"I agree," Jase put in. "This is a total embarrassment."

His daughter shrugged, then looked over at Nancy. "I guess we can both kiss that good-conduct medal good-bye, huh?"

"And the neatness medal," Nancy added. Then she snickered.

Jase had to bite his lip to keep from laughing. The idea of either of the girls getting a prize for neatness when they had food in their hair was ludicrous. Valerie, he could tell, was hiding a grin by bowing her head.

They might have survived the moment if Lily hadn't woken up and looked around right then. "Nanny!" she called out, pointing at her older sister. "Finger-paints? Momma, can I finger-paint too?"

The room erupted in laughter. But their mirth was short-lived, cut off abruptly when Mr. Reynolds pushed open his office door without warning. "I'm glad you all think this is amusing," he said. "But I assure you, it's very serious."

"I'm sorry, Mr. Reynolds," Millicent said. "We know it's serious. It's just that my three-year-old said something funny, and . . ."

The principal looked down his nose disapprovingly.

"We're sorry too," Nancy said, coming to the rescue.

"Yeah, real sorry," Valerie joined in. "It won't ever happen again, we promise."

"It had better not," he said. "As it is, I'm going to suspend you both for three days."

"But that means we'll miss—" Valerie started to object, but Jase sent her a hard look that silenced her. The girls were getting off easy, in his opinion.

After the details of the suspension were worked out, Jase was more than happy to clear out of that office. They all walked out together, toward the front entrance of the school and the parking lot.

The girls got their share of stares, but no one said anything.

Once they were outside, Jase sent Valerie ahead to the car. Nancy ran ahead, too, holding Lily by the hand, giving Jase and Millicent a few seconds of privacy.

Jase intended to take advantage of it. "You think we handled it well?"

She expelled a deep breath. "I don't know. I'm still shocked all the way to my toes. Nancy's never gotten into trouble before."

"Neither has Valerie. Did you mean what you said back there?"

"What did I say?" she asked warily.

"That if you wanted to see me, you'd see me. And if you wanted to kiss—"

She held up a hand. "I remember. Yes, I meant it. I'm not going to let my daughter dictate to me. But there's still that 'if.' "

"Ah, I see. You know, if you don't put your foot down now about this dating thing, you'll be letting Nancy get the upper hand. Not a good precedent." He held his breath, wondering if Millicent would buy the it's-for-your-own-good theory.

Millicent gave him an appraising look, her eyes gleaming with suspicion. "Nancy was right about one thing."

"What's that?"

"You're confusing me. Big time."

FIVE

Millicent felt good and truly hoodwinked. How had she let Jase talk her into such a ridiculous agreement, to go on a date for the sake of maintaining maternal control over Nancy?

His rationale had sounded so sensible in the school parking lot. Now, a week and a half later, as she stood in front of her bathroom mirror applying her seldom-worn makeup with a trembling hand, the arguments he'd used seemed ludicrous. Nancy wasn't going to stop her from doing whatever she wanted to do, this week or next year.

Then again, even now Nancy was having a first-class pout about her mother going out on a *date*. She had recruited Will to her cause, and she had used some pretty heavy-duty arguments of her own. One of them, "How could you do this to Daddy?" had given Millicent pause.

Still, she hadn't called Jase to cancel their outing, despite being tempted. She couldn't fall prey to Nancy's emotional blackmail. She and Jase were going to an early movie, then out for pizza. It wasn't as if they were planning to check into a sleazy motel, for heaven's sake. She'd told Becky, who'd volunteered to baby-sit again, that she would be home by ten. There was nothing wrong with her going out on a causal date with a friend.

She sighed. Some friend. He hadn't felt like a friend when she'd kissed him.

Not that she intended to repeat *that* performance, she thought as she twisted her hair up into a butterfly clip. She'd been emotionally fragile that day, that was all—seeing Lana and Sloan married, thinking about Theodora. She felt stronger now.

Her confidence wavered only slightly when Jase appeared at her front door looking lean, tan, and rugged in crisp jeans and a polo shirt. He needed a haircut, she noticed. That dashing shock of dark hair that habitually flopped over his forehead was threatening his eyes. But the longish hair only added to that untamed aura she associated with him.

Funny, he was a respected neurologist, a widowed father of three. What could be more proper? Yet when he looked at her, his burning gaze was anything but proper. Worse, it made *her* feel a bit on the untamed side herself.

After greeting Millicent and Becky, Jase went immediately to Mary Jane. The baby was seated in her wind-up swing in the living room, and Jase began a low-pitched conversation with her, letting her grab at his fingers, shaking her rattle, responding to her coos of delight. Millicent had never seen a man so at ease with small children. Lily was drawn to him, too, vying for his attention, trying to get him to look at her new picture book.

"I'll read your book, precious," Becky said. "Mommy and Dr. Jase will be late for their movie if they don't get a move on." She shot a meaningful glance at Millicent.

Lily, sensing her mother's imminent departure, toddled across the room and attached herself to Millicent's leg, then started a shrill ruckus.

"Now, Lily, you're going to be a good girl for Aunt Becky, aren't you?" Millicent swung her daughter up into her arms.

"Don't go, don't go!" Lily screamed.

Even Lily was getting into the guilt and manipulation game.

Becky came to the rescue. "Come to Aunt Becky, angel. You want to play with your baby sister?"

"Mar' Jane?" Lily was immediately distracted. She'd been fascinated with the baby since her arrival, and only a little jealous.

"That's right," Becky said, easing Lily away from Millicent. "Let's show Mary Jane your new book. We can read it to her together."

Mollified, Lily immediately wound her arms around Becky's neck.

"I think we'd better make our escape now," Millicent stage-whispered to Jase, who was watching the performance with amusement and sympathy. "Do you have to face this with Ginger?"

"Every time I walk out the door for the hospital," he said as he rose, giving Mary Jane a parting tickle under her chubby chin.

Millicent called a farewell to her two older children, who were hibernating in their rooms in protest. They didn't answer, but she hadn't really expected them to. Then she went to Mary Jane, kissed her on the cheek, and nearly sprinted to the door. She still had a hard time being separated from her youngest, especially with the baby's health a question mark.

The pediatrician still wasn't satisfied. A battery of tests were scheduled for later this week. That was another reason she'd agreed to go out with Jase, though. If there was one person who could distract her from her problems, he was it. Never mind that he was a whole new set of problems.

The evening was balmy, breezy—way too romantic. Summer was approaching with audacious speed. The kids were already out of school. Another week and it would be June.

"You look pretty," Jase said casually as they walked out the door together.

"Thank you." Silly that a simple compliment would make her blush. But it did. She could feel the heat rising in her cheeks. She'd never thought of herself as pretty or beautiful. Ronnie had thought her clever. Capable. Generous. But he'd never made a big deal of the way she looked. No one had.

Jase opened the car door for her. She'd been expecting a typical doctor's conveyance—a Jaguar, maybe a BMW. But once she saw it, she decided the roomy four-door sedan probably suited a man with kids better than some flashy sports car.

Things would be easier, she decided, if Jase weren't so darn steady. If he was a cad, or a womanizer, or just a little bit unsavory, she could convince herself that she didn't want him around her kids and be done with this whole business. Problem was, she couldn't find anything wrong with him. The fact that he oozed animal magnetism, that he made her think of jungle heat and tropical breezes and thunderstorms, didn't constitute a fault.

"How's Mary Jane doing?" Jase asked, as he always did. She couldn't blame him for having a special interest in the only baby he'd ever delivered.

Still, tonight, she'd rather the question did not come up. "Fine, just fine," she said unconvincingly. "You saw her. She's a happy baby. Hardly ever cries."

"She seems very bright and alert," he agreed. "She has good color too. But you mentioned a problem the other day."

"I did?" Oh, yes. That was when the "problem" was only a vague suspicion. Mentioning it to Jase, minimizing it, had given the possibility of illness fewer sharp teeth with which to gnaw at her. She'd convinced herself it was nothing to worry about.

Now, however, she got a knot in her stomach

the size of a potato every time she thought of those stupid tests.

"Your pediatrician noticed something?" he prompted.

She might as well tell Jase, she decided, although she hadn't mentioned it to anyone else. " 'Developmental anomalies,' Dr. Daas called it. Dull reflexes on one side. Some weakness. She said it was nothing to panic about." Yet. Wait until the test results.

"Are you following up?" Jase asked. She could tell he was trying to make the question sound casual, but there was a definite edge to his voice.

"Tests," Millicent answered, her voice flat. "Friday. But she seems fine to me. Babies are supposed to be weak, aren't they?" Desperation had crept into her question.

Jase sighed. "Sometimes a trained eye can see what even the most caring, attentive mother can't."

And whose eye was more trained than Jase's? "You saw something, didn't you?" It was an accusation rather than a question.

"Yeah," he admitted. "Or I thought I did. It's very subtle. But tests are a good idea. I was going to suggest it if your pediatrician hadn't."

"What do you think it could be?" she asked.

"Oh, Millicent, I couldn't even hazard a guess without doing a thorough examination. Even then—"

"Don't stonewall me! That's exactly what Dr. Daas said. Or didn't say."

He laid a gentle hand on her arm, then her shoulder. "That's because there are a million and one possible reasons behind the symptoms you mentioned. It would be irresponsible for any doctor to guess at this point."

"Then as a friend, couldn't you throw out some possibilities? Best-case and worst-case scenarios?" To her horror, hot tears pressed against the backs of her eyes. She swallowed, sniffed, blinked, but the tears spilled out of her eyes and down her cheeks. She was crying, and the car wasn't even out of her driveway yet.

Good heavens, she hadn't cried at all about Mary Jane's condition until now. She'd thought she was handling it well. But apparently she'd been holding a few emotions at bay. What a pity Jase had to be the one to witness her breakdown.

Would the poor man ever see her at anything but her worst?

"Maybe we better forget about this," she said through her sniffles. "As you can see, I'm not really up for socializing, and I don't think I could sit through a movie." She'd just reached for the door handle when Jase hit the gas, ruining her chances of escape.

"We won't go to a movie, then," he said, perfectly relaxed as his respectable sedan fishtailed in her gravel driveway, then rumbled over the newly rebuilt bridge. Didn't anything flap the man? Most men she knew would do anything to escape from a blubbering female. On the few occasions when she'd cried in front of Ronnie, he'd transformed into a fidgeting, blithering idiot, mouthing trite condolences.

"Then where are we going?"

"How about my house?"

"Oh, I couldn't! No, your children can't see me—"

"They're not home. They've gone up to Dallas to visit their grandparents for a couple of weeks, now that school is out."

"But Saundra—"

"Is visiting her cousin in Waco. We'll have the place to ourselves. I'll pamper you. We can dig up something for dinner, open a bottle of wine—"

"And you'll tell me what might be wrong with my baby?" she pressed. He had to have some thoughts on the subject. Even if those thoughts were pure conjecture, she wanted to know what they were. Knowledge was power.

He sighed. "All right, all right, I'll share some ideas with you, although it goes against my better judgment."

"Jase, nothing could be worse than the things I've cooked up in my imagination." Which was true. Lying alone in bed at night, she'd stared up into the darkness and pictured her precious daughter in a wheelchair, or an invalid for life. She'd even relived Ronnie's funeral, substituting a tiny white coffin for the large walnut one he'd been buried in.

She was in the habit of picturing the worst. But until tonight, it hadn't really come home to her what it would mean if Mary Jane had a serious illness. She hadn't truly comprehended how frightened she was until moments before.

Nothing more was said on the drive to Jase's house. Millicent took in the elegance of the neighborhood, the size of the homes. Unlike his car, his home didn't surprise her. It was where a doctor should live, a red-bricked, white-columned almost-mansion that screamed wealth and respectability.

"Your home is lovely," she murmured as he pushed the button on the garage door opener.

"Thanks. I always thought it was too big, but those three pack rats of mine seem to have filled it up."

"I know what you mean. Even with all the add-ons we built, I still had to crowd Mary Jane's nursery into my sewing room. When she gets bigger, she and Lily will have to share." If she gets bigger. Millicent swallowed the lump in her throat. "That, or maybe I can move my pottery back to the barn where I used to have it."

"Pottery. That's why you were all smudged up that day in the principal's office. I'd been wondering . . ."

"It's how I make my living."

"You never told me you were an artist."

She shrugged. Over the past few years she'd enjoyed moderate success with her ceramics. She'd pioneered a unique type of cracked-glaze finish that was now being imitated by potters as far away as the Midwest. But she'd been out of touch with her artistic, creative side lately. Even that day she'd been interrupted by the principal's call, she'd only been playing around with her clay, hoping for inspiration.

"I haven't been doing much since the baby, but I've got to get back into it," she said. "Changing diapers doesn't pay the bills."

"I admire you."

"Good heavens, why?"

"I could never be self-employed. I'm afraid I'd sleep the day away. That's why I like being on staff at the hospital."

She didn't tell him that sleeping alone in her bed held little appeal anymore. She spent far too many hours staring at the ceiling, feeling sorry for herself or wondering if she could have done anything differently. Sometimes thinking the unthinkable.

"You don't strike me as the slightest bit lazy, Jase," she said.

He cocked one eyebrow and gave her a crooked smile. "You've never seen me on a Sunday morning, loafing over coffee and the paper. You can't budge me off the sofa with a crowbar."

The picture he painted was appealing despite his self-deprecating tone. She saw him in soft gray sweatpants, shirtless, his face shadowed with yesterday's beard, his hair tousled. . . .

An ache rose up in her from nowhere. Oh, Lord, not only did she see him, but she saw *herself* in the picture, wearing a sexy robe from Victoria's

Secret—the kind she'd never owned—snuggled next to him on the sofa, absorbed in a paperback, reaching over to touch his chest every so often. . . .

"Millicent? You okay?"

Jolted back to the present, she stumbled through her assurances that she was fine, just had a lot on her mind. An awful lot. "You know," she said, "I'm feeling okay now. We could do the movie."

"We'd be late for it now. Anyway, I've got scads of videotapes. Anything from Charlie Chaplin to *Bill and Ted's Excellent Adventure*. I even have popcorn."

"Okay, okay, you sold me." They both got out of the car and into his house. His empty, secluded, private house. And suddenly Millicent was afraid—not of him, because she knew he would never force himself on her. She was afraid of herself, the woman with the lascivious thoughts and impulsive actions.

Earlier she'd thought she was feeling stronger. But she wasn't. She felt as vulnerable as a blind newborn kitten.

To his credit, Jase said and did everything right. He cheered her, got her to talking about silly things, regaled her with stories about his own kids. The dinner he provided was distinctly unromantic—macaroni and cheese at the kitchen table, root beer to drink, all on Flintstones placemats.

"I never said I could cook," he apologized. "Except steaks. If there'd been a couple of steaks in the fridge—"

"Say no more. My pantry is in much worse shape than yours. If I'd been asked to prepare a dinner for you on the spur of the moment, you would have been treated to peanut butter and juice boxes."

"I crave adult food sometimes, right along with adult conversation." He touched her hand and gazed into her eyes, and she saw a familiar yearning there. Like looking into a mirror.

Quickly he pulled away, as if he'd forgotten himself for a moment. His eyes closed, and when he opened them they were once again just normal hazel eyes, sincere and friendly but nothing more.

She realized then that he was putting forth considerable effort to keep this evening on friendly, nonsexual terms. Was it because he feared she would kiss him again the way she had at the lake if he gave her even the slightest opening?

And if that was what he feared, were his fears legitimate? She found herself more often than not staring at his mouth, remembering how it had felt against hers, hard yet gentle, warm, commanding. Her stomach fluttered as if a tiny bird were trapped inside.

She helped Jase clear the table, careful to keep her distance so that they didn't inadvertently touch. If he touched her again, she might shatter into fragments the way a badly glazed pot shattered in her kiln.

"You said something about wine?" she asked brightly when the kitchen was spotless. Wine would relax her, she figured, and she needed relaxing. That, or she was going to resort to one of those tranquilizers her doctor had prescribed shortly after Ronnie's death.

Because she'd discovered she was pregnant the day after the funeral, she'd never taken those pills—not even one. But she'd kept them with her at all times, like a security blanket, just in case.

"Now there's something adult we can safely indulge in," he said. "White or red?"

"Red," she said automatically, her mind mulling over the alternatives, the other "adult" behavior that *wouldn't* be safe. "And didn't you say something about videos? I could use a mindless adventure movie, James Bond or something. But no popcorn. I'm full." She was babbling. She never babbled.

Before she knew what was happening, Jase had hustled her into a den, which was cozily cluttered with the stuff girl children generate, along with a few grown-up male things too—a pair of athletic shoes, a worn tennis racquet leaning in one corner, some model antique cars idling on a desk.

A large TV dominated the room, and Millicent found herself on a cushy couch, her feet up, a glass of red wine in her hand. Jase seated himself a more-than-decent distance from her. He took what looked like a fortifying gulp of wine. "You wanted to talk about Mary Jane," he said.

Millicent sploshed some of her wine on the leg of her khaki trousers. She'd forgotten. For a little while she'd forgotten. The realization filled her with guilt. "Please," she said.

"All right." He sighed, cleared his throat, and jumped in with both feet. "The symptoms I observed in Mary Jane could be nothing more than a delay in the development of her nervous system. It could cure itself and never give you a another moment's worry. But," he hastened to add before she could express any kind of relief, "the symptoms could also indicate any number of more serious conditions."

"Go on," she forced herself to say when he paused. "What conditions?"

"Well, she could have sustained a head injury of which you're unaware—even a small bump on the head can be devastating to a newborn."

Millicent gripped the wineglass more tightly. Had Mary Jane ever fallen? Not that she could recall.

"Or," Jase continued, "it could be a vascular problem—not enough oxygenated blood getting to the part of her brain that controls the left side of her body."

"Is that treatable?" she asked, fighting down panic, trying to remind herself that she'd begged him for this information.

"Sometimes."

"Okay. What else?"

He didn't look at her, and she knew the worst was yet to come. She also knew he would level with her.

"It could be a growth, in her brain or on her spine."

"You mean a tumor? Like c-cancer?" Before she could answer, the wineglass shattered in her grip. The ruby red liquid spilled into her lap and splashed on the sofa, followed by drops of her own blood. She stared numbly at the cut on her palm, feeling no pain.

"Holy— Millicent!" He was at her side in an instant, taking the fragments of glass from her and carelessly dropping them onto the carpet.

"I stained your couch." Her own voice sounded distant to her, as if she were hearing it through a tunnel.

"Forget the damn couch. I'm worried about you. Let's go into the bathroom and wash this thing out. There may still be some glass in there." He helped her to her feet.

She was wobbly. He had to hold her up until she found her balance. "I barely touched the wine," she said. "Honest."

"The sight of blood makes a lot of people woozy," he said. "This way." He ushered her into a luxurious bathroom off the den. She noticed silly, insignificant things—like how thick and lush the yellow towels looked. She needed to buy some nice, new towels for herself.

Jase ran cold water over her injured hand. The coolness felt good. His hand around her wrist, strong and sure, felt good too. So did the warmth from his body where he brushed against her, even though she was sure he didn't mean to.

When he turned off the water, he frowned. "You're still bleeding. I think you should go get the hand stitched up."

"No," Millicent said with a feeling close to panic. Emergency rooms gave her the willies. "Look, the bleeding is slowing down. Let's just bandage it up. If it doesn't stop by tomorrow, I'll go to the hospital then. I mean, I have my own personal doctor right here. You'll fix it right."

His frown deepened. "If you insist. But I'm going to disinfect the heck out of that cut, and you won't like me anymore."

"Do your worst." The idea of physical pain didn't bother her in the least. Or so she thought, until the antiseptic hit raw flesh. She flinched and squeaked.

"Told you. Take a deep breath."

She did. The pain eased. He sat her down on the commode while he wrapped sterile gauze tightly around her hand and taped it into place with practiced efficiency. When he was done, he covered her injured hand with both of his, as if his touch could heal her.

"I'm sorry if I upset you," he said.

"Please don't apologize. I dragged that information out of you against your will. And don't think I haven't imagined things just as horrible as you've described. But to hear it spelled out . . . could it be some kind of cancer? Really?"

"Millicent, I—"

"Don't stop now. I have to know."

She could tell he resented her putting him in this uncomfortable position. But this was her child they were talking about. She couldn't back down now.

He took a deep breath before saying anything else, and when he did speak, his voice was low, soothing, belying the terrible truth he told her. "If there is a tumor—and that's a big 'if'—it could be benign, or it could be malignant. But even benign tumors can create all kinds of havoc."

"She would have to have surgery," Millicent murmured. "Oh God, she's so tiny, so fragile. How could she survive it?" The tears came again. She'd thought she was stronger than this. But no matter how she tried, she could not stop the tidal wave of despair washing over her, drowning her in pain and misery.

Almost without her realizing it, Jase sat on the edge of the tub and shifted her into his lap. He wrapped his arms around her, giving her a warm envelope of security. She cried against his soft knit shirt while he petted and soothed her.

"It's so unfair," she said between wracking sobs, knowing she sounded like a sulky little girl. "With Ronnie, I knew h-he was in a risky profession. I knew there was always a ch-chance that he would walk out the door and never come back, and one day he d-did just that. But a child . . . I guess I'm really overreacting." She dissolved again, feeling utterly wretched.

"No one is ever prepared for a child's illness," Jase said. "I've dealt with a lot of parents—scared, panicked, angry, grieving. It's normal to feel this way. I just wish I could do something, say something, to help."

"Just hold me," she whispered. "As long as you're holding on to me, I can't fly into a million pieces."

Just hold me. This scene was hauntingly familiar to Jase. Libby had been so scared when her illness had been diagnosed. And for the first time in a very long time, she'd turned to him, opened up to him . . . needed him. He'd held her the same way while she'd cried, and he'd promised her he would help her, heal her, make everything better. He remembered thinking that perhaps the tenacious infection that had ravaged her body was a blessing in disguise, a new beginning for them.

But it had been the beginning of the end. Jase's promises had turned to ashes, Libby's faith to bitterness. Then suddenly she was gone.

He was very, very careful not to make any promises to Millicent. He couldn't even bring himself to be optimistic. He knew too little about Mary Jane's condition to offer any reliable opinion. Or maybe it was because he felt almost as disturbed as Millicent by the prospect of a serious illness. Mary

Jane was special to him. He'd been the very first to hold her, to welcome her to the world.

One thing he did know. Holding Millicent in his arms was sweet torture. Whether by design or by accident, she smelled like baby powder. Her whole body trembled as she cried, evoking every protective instinct he'd ever possessed and then some. But those weren't the only instincts coming to life. He was fully aroused and aware of every burning inch of contact between himself and this woman who had quickly become so precious to him.

Eventually the storm of her crying passed and she quieted. Jase fully expected her to stiffen and pull away from him, embarrassed. Instead she surprised him by relaxing against him, her whole body going warm and liquid.

Whereas she'd clung to him like a frightened child before, now her hands were engaged in a different activity.

She was caressing him.

Maybe she wasn't doing it consciously, but she was running her fingertips lightly over his arms and shoulders, his neck, exploring . . . exciting.

He had to put a stop to it. She probably had no idea what she was doing to him. But words wouldn't come. He wanted to enjoy her nearness for a few more minutes. It had been a long time, so long, since he'd experienced a woman's softness. . . .

No, that wasn't it. Even if he'd been with a different woman every night of his life, he would still want Millicent Jones. He stroked her hair and cursed the circumstances. Her misfortune had brought her to him, but would it forever be a barrier between them?

"Feel better?" he finally asked her.

"Um. Not better, exactly. Just drained." She kept her face pressed firmly against his shoulder so that her words were muffled. He could feel the warmth of her breath through his shirt. "Like someone pulled out my plug and emptied me."

He was familiar enough with that feeling.

"Think we can go back into the den now and find a more comfortable place to sit?" he asked, reluctantly loosening his hold on her.

Millicent, however, clung to him even more tenaciously. "No, don't let go of me, not yet," she said, almost desperately. She turned her tearstained face up to him, and the fierceness in her doe's eyes nearly undid him.

She needed him.

"I'm not normally this—"

"Don't apologize. You're allowed to do whatever you want or need to do when you're with me, no questions asked. I'm not about to judge you. I did some pretty crazy things after Libby died."

"Crazy? This crazy?"

It seemed as natural as breathing when their lips came together. Like warm honey poured on buttered toast. Again her actions took him by surprise. But unlike the kiss at the lake, born out of anger and defiance, this one was pure passion and deep hunger. Powerless to do anything except react, he kissed her back, cupping her head in his hand, drinking her in, taking everything she had to give.

It wasn't enough. He'd never wanted to possess a woman the way he did Millicent. He felt greedy for even thinking about his own needs when she was hurting so badly. But his hunger was overpowering. He was drunk with it.

From somewhere deep inside he retained a fragment of sanity. When he found himself stroking her breasts through her thin silk blouse, and he heard the soft, mewling noises of approval she made, felt her nipples peaking into tight pebbles, he struggled to grab on to that sliver of sanity for all he was worth. Struggled and failed. The desire was stronger than anything he'd experienced before.

She started unbuttoning his shirt with her good hand. The touch of her cool fingertips against hot skin was almost more than he could bear. He shuddered with pleasure. He knew he should stop this, but he knew, as surely as he knew the color of Millicent's eyes, that they were going to make love. And if he didn't do something quickly, they were going to make love right there in the bathroom.

"I feel so empty," she whispered urgently. "Fill me back up, please. Please." She punctuated her plea with another searing kiss.

Jase stood and scooped her into his arms. The bedroom. Could they make it to the bedroom?

SIX

Millicent felt the floor drop out from under her. It took her a moment to realize Jase had picked her up and was carrying her out the door.

What have I done? she thought briefly, a flutter of panic starting inside her rib cage. But she smacked the objection down along with the panic. She needed this. She couldn't call a halt to it now, even if she'd wanted to.

She never opened her eyes, never looked at the rest of the house that was no doubt slipping past her. She felt herself going up the stairs in Jase's arms. Jase's footsteps on the treads were strong and sure, and he carried her with seeming effortlessness.

He paused on the top landing and, with a low groan, kissed her again. There was no mistaking the passion. His desire was real, not part of some fantasy she'd built. It made her dizzy to think that she, plain ol' Millicent, had inspired this heated response.

With their lips still touching, Jase started walking again. He nudged open a door at the end of the hall and carried her into a darkened room. His bedroom.

There really was no turning back.

Don't think about it, she silently commanded herself. She didn't want to think, she just wanted to feel. And the feeling that vaulted through in front of apprehension, guilt, and fear, was white-hot anticipation. She knew she could lose herself in Jase, at least for a while. If ever a woman needed to lose herself . . .

He set her down gently, and for a moment they simply stood close, breathing in time with each other. Then she started to unbutton her blouse.

By the faint glow of silvery moonlight drifting through the window, she could see that his gaze was glued to her hands, to her fumbling efforts. Her right hand, wrapped in gauze, was about as useful as a bear's paw.

Jase stilled her hands with his. "I'll do that."

He finished the buttons, then slipped his fingers beneath the shirt and slid it off her shoulders. His warm hands lingered on her arms, and she shivered with pleasure.

He guided her to the bed—it was big and soft, she noticed with a weird sort of detachment. "Don't move," he said, the hoarse urgency in his voice making her shiver again. He went to the dresser and rummaged around in the top drawer. She could barely see him in the semidarkness, but she was glad he hadn't turned on a light. Darkness seemed appropriate for their liaison.

"What are you doing?" she asked a little forlornly, missing his touch and the illusion of security it gave her. Without it she was in danger of thinking again.

"Condoms," he muttered. "Between us we have seven children. I'm assuming you don't want to try for eight. Where did I put the damn things?"

"Oh." She'd never in her life given any thought to birth control, which was one reason she had four kids. Jase was being so thoughtful. If he was any kinder, any more gentle, she was going to cry again. She didn't want to be treated like some porcelain doll.

"Eureka," he said, and slammed the dresser drawer. Then he was beside her again. "Now, where were we?"

He tried to go slow, and she appreciated the effort because she knew it was for her sake, but slow wasn't what she wanted this night. Fast and hard, so she wouldn't have time to think—about anything.

She tugged at his belt, at the hem of his shirt, craving bare skin against bare skin. The more anxious she became, the more futile her efforts grew.

"Millie. Easy, love."

Love. Somewhere in the back of her passion-fogged brain, she knew love should be a part of what they were doing. Was it here? Even a little?

Then she stopped worrying about it, because Jase had gotten himself naked, and all she could think about was touching, being touched, letting his warmth and compassion for her blot out everything else.

Her slacks joined the heap of clothes on the floor. She jerked the rest of her things off, unwilling to postpone this event one second longer. It was as if she were afraid someone would take it away from her if she didn't grab for the brass ring immediately.

"Be with me now, Jase."

"But, Millicent—"

"I can't wait. Please."

"I'm afraid I'll hurt you." Nevertheless, he lay down beside her. He stroked her the way he would a nervous cat.

She realized that in her desperation she was probably scaring him to death. She took a deep breath. He wasn't going anywhere.

He kissed her again while his hands continued to stroke, caress, explore. She tightened with glorious expectancy when he touched her lightly between her legs, then again when he slid a finger inside. She was slick, ready.

He was ready too. No doubt about that. She opened to him, urging him to lie in the cradle of her thighs.

His entrance was surprisingly painful, and she bit her lip. She remembered then that her obstetrician hadn't given her the green light to have intercourse. The subject simply hadn't come up. But the pain subsided almost immediately, replaced by a delicious friction as Jase moved slowly in and out, filling her, reaching for all those empty places inside her.

She would have no regrets about this, she promised herself.

The pace quickly accelerated. Millicent moaned her pleasure. Jase whispered her name, burying his face in her hair. His voice sent her over the edge to some other dimension, one of peace and utter fulfillment. There was no room for anything else. Millicent felt overwhelmed by the emotions welling up.

Yes, it was there. She detected a seed of love. Not the frying-pan-to-the-head kind she'd felt the moment she'd laid eyes on Ronnie, but still very real, waiting to take root and be nurtured.

The realization should have frightened her into a coma. What business did she have falling in love? But she was actually more relieved than scared. The knowledge that love played some part in this intimacy made it okay, at least a little bit. She laughed and cried at the same time. Her pleasure bloomed like a late summer rose, pushing against her skin from the inside, threatening to make her explode.

And then she did explode. The intensity of her climax took her by surprise. There was nothing in her experience to prepare her for the rolling waves of ecstasy that kept crashing over her like a sea at storm crest.

Jase found his release. He was less flamboyant about it than she'd been, but even in her dazed condition she could see the delight he took in her, the utter peace of finding that perfect place on a mystical plane.

Afterward they lay together for a long time. Jase continued to stroke her softly, as if to reassure himself she was real. Finally he drew away from her, raised up to pull the chain on the ceiling fan above the bed, then lay back down beside her.

"Put your head on my shoulder," he whispered.

She complied, snuggling closer, knowing she had only a little time left on this special island they'd created from need and desperation and pure thin air.

She'd been right. Making love had kept her devilish fears at bay, at least for a while.

When next she became aware, she realized they'd dozed off. That familiar trickle of panic reasserted itself, moving from her chest to wiggle up and down her spine and prickle her scalp. How long had they been asleep? She eased away from Jase, who slept blissfully, and stepped into the bathroom to freshen up. Only then did she dare look at her watch.

She threw the bathroom door open. "Jase!" she cried. "Jase, wake up!"

He sat up, rubbing his eyes. "Hmmm?"

"Wake up! I have to go."

Instantly his eyes flew open. "What's wrong?"

"I have to go," she repeated as she rooted

around on the floor for her clothes. "I told Becky I'd be home before ten, and it's almost midnight!" She tried to put both feet through the same leg of her panties. Cursing under her breath, she righted the obstinate undergarment. Her bra strap got twisted as she hastily donned it, but she didn't fix that.

"Why don't you call Becky and tell her we're on our way? Then we don't have to rush," Jase suggested sensibly.

"No, let's just go." She supposed she was postponing the inevitable explanation she would make to Becky. Millicent was never late. Becky would take one look at her and know what had happened.

Millicent hadn't considered that before. Lying next to Jase, trying to reconcile this very un-Millicentlike behavior, she'd been pretty sure she could live with what she and Jase had done. But for anyone else to know that she'd forsaken Ronnie's memory so soon after his death, after the birth of his child . . . that was something else again. The thought sobered her as nothing else could.

Somehow Jase managed to finish dressing before she did. He was running a comb through his hair while she was still crawling around on the floor looking for her right shoe.

Suddenly he was behind her, grasping her by the shoulders. "Millicent, get a grip. Your shoe is in your hand."

"I know that," she said impatiently. "I'm looking for the other one."

"It's on your foot."

"Oh."

He helped her up. Then with a sigh he said, "I was afraid this would happen."

"What? That we'd fall asleep?"

"That you would be upset afterward. You are, aren't you?"

"I'm not upset!" She knew her denial was a little too hot, but his sympathy grated on her right now. "I just hate being late, that's all."

"No regrets?"

"Ah . . ." She couldn't meet his all-too-knowing gaze. "No regrets."

"You're not a very good liar, Millicent," he said, though the words didn't sound as if they'd been intended to sting. "You probably wouldn't be normal if you didn't have some misgivings. I'm feeling a little funny myself. I didn't expect to, but there it is, staring me in the face."

"Really?" She hadn't even considered that. She'd never thought about men having qualms where sex was concerned. "Am I the first—" She cut herself off, realizing how rude the question was.

He answered her anyway. "No. Early on I had some meaningless flings. I was trying to forget, to blot out the . . . the . . . Well, anyway, this is a lot different." *For me, anyway.* He hadn't said the words, but they floated unspoken on thought waves.

She didn't ask how the experience was different from his previous flings. She wasn't ready to hear the answer.

Perhaps sensing her reluctance, he didn't elaborate.

"I'm okay with this, really." She managed a smile, for his sake, because she didn't want him worrying about her. "But I have to get home."

They made the drive back to her house in almost total silence. It was definitely awkward. Millicent stared out the window into the night, willing her mind to quiet, willing that kernel of panic to go away. What would happen now? Had she alienated Jase with her mad rush to escape? Or was he relieved, having satisifed his curiosity about making love? Was he perhaps disappointed? She didn't think of herself as particularly artful or clever in bed. She just did whatever came naturally. Ronnie had never complained—he'd always seemed to enjoy himself a lot, in fact—but he'd never referred to her as a tigress or temptress or anything like that.

Jase didn't give her even a small clue.

"I'll come in with you if you want," he said as he pulled into her driveway. "I'll tell Becky it's my fault you're late."

"No, but thanks," Millicent said quickly. It would only make it that much worse if Becky saw the two of them together. "Becky won't be mad or anything. It's just that she has to get up early for work tomorrow, and I don't like taking advantage of her."

"Will you at least give my apologies to Becky along with yours?"

"Yes, of course. Jase, you don't have to walk me

to the door," she said when he unfastened his seat belt. "After all, we aren't in high school."

He rolled his eyes and opened his car door anyway. "I've never in my life dumped a woman in her driveway after a date, and I'm not starting now. What in the world makes you think it's some kind of chore?"

"Sorry," she mumbled. "I think that's my insecurities showing. It might take me a while to get the hang of this . . . dating thing."

Instantly his face was transformed by an indulgent smile. "You're doing fine, Millicent."

"Oh, yeah. I start the evening by getting hysterical, then I break one of your wineglasses, bleed all over your bathroom—"

"You gave me the most incredible couple of hours of my life," he interrupted. "Seems that way, anyhow."

Suddenly she felt much better. All she'd needed, she realized, was some validation, some indication that *he* wasn't plagued by regrets.

"I know what you mean," she said, her voice thick. She reached across the void between them and stroked his cheek, then quickly climbed out of the car before she succumbed to any more foolish tears.

Their good-night was brief, awkwardness creeping up on them again. Jase kissed her, fast and hard. He tucked a strand of her hair behind her ear, opened the front door for her, then vanished into the midnight darkness.

Becky was asleep on the couch.

Good, Millicent thought. Maybe she could hustle her sister out of the house without her knowing what time it was. She dreaded facing up to her latest indiscretion. Having her daughter witness that kiss was bad enough.

But first there was another priority. Millicent tiptoed through the living room, down the hall, and to the nursery. By the glow of the night light she could see that Mary Jane was sleeping peacefully on her tummy. Millicent resisted the urge to pick her up and hold her close. The baby needed every bit of rest and strength she could get to fight whatever illness was attacking her.

Somehow Millicent knew it wasn't just "nothing." There was something wrong. With a mother's instinct she could feel it all the way down to her bones.

But for now Mary Jane was safe and happy.

Millicent peeked in on her other angels—all of them in blissful dreamland—before returning to the living room.

Becky was stirring. She sat up, stretched, and immediately checked her watch. "Oh, my." She looked around, caught sight of Millicent, and blushed. "How long did you let me sleep?"

It was so tempting. But Millicent didn't dare stretch the truth any more than she had to. "I don't know. I just got home a few minutes ago myself. I didn't mean to be so late." She busied herself cleaning up toys from the floor and dropping them into a big net caddie she kept in the corner behind a lamp table. "Jase and I were having such a good time, we lost track of the hour."

"So you had fun! That's great. How did you . . . Millicent, what happened to your hand?"

"I broke a glass. It's not as serious as the bandage would indicate, but Jase felt bad about it. I think he'd have wrapped me up like a mummy if I'd let him."

"Mmm, that's what I call first aid," Becky said on a sigh. "How did you like the movie?"

Oh, shoot. What movie had they been planning to see? Millicent thought furiously, couldn't remember, and so threw up her hands. "We never made it to the movie. We got to talking and decided to skip it."

"Mm-hmm. Sounds like you had a *really* good time."

"Now, Becky, don't make more of this than is there. He's a great guy. We found a lot of things to talk about, a lot of things in common." Like great sex.

Oh Lord, she had to stop thinking naughty thoughts like that! She'd made her choices and now she had to live with them, but that didn't mean she had to go on making foolish choices. Besides the fact that she did not want a heavy relationship at this point in her life, it wasn't fair to take advantage of Jase just because he was handy and willing.

Millicent combed nervous fingers through her hair, only then realizing she'd lost her butterfly clip somewhere along the way. It was probably in Jase's bed, where his housekeeper or one of the kids would find it.

Becky eyed her big sister speculatively. "A lot of things in common. Mm-hmm."

"Stop saying that!"

"What?" Becky asked with exaggerated innocence. "I'm agreeing with you. Do you think you'll go out with him again?"

"Jase?" Duh! Who else would she be talking about? "I honestly don't know. I'm not really ready for this dating thing, you know. It hasn't even been a year—"

"There's nothing magic about twelve months, you know." She proceeded cautiously with her next bit of advice, hesitating between words. "Ronnie . . . wouldn't have wanted you . . . moping around because of him."

"And then there are the kids," Millicent continued sensibly. "They're appalled at the idea of Mom having a . . . a boyfriend."

"So, they'll get used to the idea. They're kids, they're resilient. Listen, sis, maybe this isn't any of my business, but great guys who are crazy about you don't grow on trees, you know. I'm still looking for mine. You've been lucky enough to find two. Maybe the timing isn't ideal, but don't let Jase slip away just because of that."

"How do you know he's crazy about me?" Millicent asked, instead of arguing against her sister's eminently sensible points.

"I see it in his eyes when he looks at you. And he's so good with the kids! I'm not saying you have to marry the guy tomorrow, but don't rule him out just because of the calendar. Or because you're worried about what people will think."

"But that *is* something to consider," Millicent said, dropping into her oldest, most comfy easy chair. "If it was just me . . . But the kids. I can't let anything I do hurt them. They mean everything to me."

"Well, of course. But if you just take things one day at a time—"

"Point taken," Millicent said, a little more curtly than she intended. She was tired, and she needed to be alone to think. To savor. To decide if she'd really messed up, and if so, how badly. "I'll try not to drive him off until I'm good and sure I don't want him. Don't you need to be getting home?"

"Okay, okay, I can take a hint. Anyway, I've said my piece. The kids were dreamy, no problems." Becky shouldered her backpack. Without further conversation she accepted the folded dollar bills Millicent handed to her. She started for the door, then apparently couldn't resist one parting shot:

"I hope he was as good as he looks."

Jase had been half expecting the phone call that whole Friday afternoon. Still, when it came, somehow he wasn't prepared.

"Jase, this is Nora Daas," the voice on the

phone said. She continued on in a no-nonsense fashion. "I have a case I'd like you to consult on. A ten-week-old baby girl with a tumor—"

"Mary Jane Jones," Jase said woodenly.

"How—how did you know that?"

"I've taken a special interest in her since her birth," he explained. "I delivered her, you know."

"Oh, yes, Millicent told me all about it. But how did you know she was the one I was talking about?"

"I knew she was having tests today. Just a feeling. So it is a tumor?" Damn. "Where?"

"In her neck. It's small, round, well-defined. I want you to look at her MRI."

"Do you think it's cancerous?" he made himself ask.

"I'm sure hoping not. We could do a biopsy, but the thing's going to have to come out no matter what. It's pressing on her spine and causing all sorts of problems. You're the one to do the surgery, of course."

"Nora, I can't."

"What? Of course you can. You're the most qualified—the *only* qualified surgeon in three counties."

"Take her up to Dallas. There are any number of capable neurosurgeons there."

"Can I ask why you won't do it?"

He supposed he owed Nora an explanation, even if he didn't feel ready to talk about his relationship with Millicent. "I'm involved with the baby's mother. It wouldn't be ethical for me to treat Mary Jane. I'm too close."

"You and Millicent Jones?" Nora said, her voice dripping with disbelief. Then, "I'm sorry, that was rude. It's just that that was the last thing I expected to hear. She's such a recent widow, and she seemed so torn up. . . . Oh, dear, I'm just making things worse. Me and my big mouth."

"It's okay. Millie and I are a little surprised by it too. But you understand my predicament. I'll be happy to take a look at the tests, but I can't be the one to operate."

"Of course, I understand. Okay if I drop by your office in a few minutes?"

"Sure. Um, Nora, have you told Millicent about the test results yet?"

"Not yet. I wanted to get your input first. She's coming in at four o'clock for the full story."

"I'd like to be there." If there was any small comfort he could offer her, he would, though he couldn't imagine anything that would soften the blow. A tumor. Surgery. On a tiny baby. He'd performed dozens of surgeries on infants with a high percentage of success, but thinking about Mary Jane going under the knife made his gut twist.

After the call was concluded, Jase continued to stare at the phone, wishing he could throw it across the room.

A damn tumor.

What had Millicent ever done to deserve this?

SEVEN

The news of Mary Jane's diagnosis barely fazed Millicent. Perhaps it was because, in her heart, she'd already known something was terribly wrong. She'd already had her reaction—at Jase's house two nights earlier.

So she accepted the news with her usual, calm stoicism. Jase was the one pacing the room like a caged tiger, looking as if he wanted to hit something. Oddly, his distress was comforting to her. She knew he cared—about her, her family, her feelings. That made what had happened between them a little less troubling, although she was still fighting that "unfaithful" pall that had draped itself over her psyche.

Nancy and Will had been giving her the silent treatment, and even Lily had been scowling at her, imitating her older siblings' disapproval.

"So, you're saying surgery is the only option?"

Millicent asked, just to be sure she'd fully understood.

"Yes," Dr. Daas answered. "I wish the news was better. Of course, you're welcome to get a second opinion—"

"And this surgery is risky?" Millicent interrupted. She didn't need any further opinions, not if Jase agreed with Dr. Daas.

"All surgery is risky," Jase said. "But Mary Jane is a strong baby. There's no reason to believe she won't come through it okay. But because the operation involves her spine, there's an added risk."

"Paralysis?" Millicent barely breathed the word as images of wheelchairs and leg braces and respirators assailed her.

"That's right," Dr. Daas said. "It's difficult to tell how invasive the tumor is until the surgeon gets in there. Hopefully it will come out clean, and there will be no problem. And although I can't make any guarantees, this particular tumor doesn't bear the characteristics of malignancy."

Millicent looked at Jase for confirmation. Not that she didn't trust her pediatrician, but she was grasping at any straws of optimism she could find.

Jase didn't meet her gaze. He was staring at a statue of a bobcat sitting on the shelf.

"I have a list of surgeons for you to choose from. Two are from Dallas, one from Tyler—"

"But I thought Jase would do the surgery," Millicent said, alarmed. "This is your specialty, right, Jase? Pediatric neurosurgery?"

Both doctors looked a little uncomfortable. "It wouldn't be appropriate for me to do the surgery, Millicent," Jase said. "I'm . . . too close to the patient. It's just not wise."

"But you delivered her!"

"I didn't know you then."

Millicent really didn't understand. Sure, Jase was acquainted with Mary Jane, but it wasn't as if she were a relative. She supposed an involvement with her implied a closeness with her children. She started to argue further, but seeing the inflexible lines of Jase's mouth, she decided it would be futile. She couldn't deny that he was fond of her daughter, she supposed. They did seem to have a special affinity for each other. The affection went two ways. Mary Jane lit up like Fourth of July whenever she set eyes on him.

Dr. Daas walked around her desk and pressed a piece of paper into Millicent's limp hand. "Here's the list of surgeons. I suggest you call each of them, maybe even go visit them. Ask lots of questions. Then choose the one you feel most comfortable with."

"They're all excellent," Jase added. "I interned with Dr. Boynton. He's brilliant."

Millicent sighed. "All right. I'll get on the phone first thing Monday morning."

"Fine. Listen, I'm late for a meeting," Dr. Daas said as she gathered up some folders, "but you two are welcome to stay in here and talk some more. Just push the lock button on the door when you leave." She gave Millicent's shoulder a sympathetic squeeze before exiting the office.

As soon as they were alone Millicent felt awkward again. She and Jase hadn't talked since that night. She'd sort of expected him to call the next day, had tensed with anticipation each time the phone had rung. But he hadn't called.

She couldn't blame him. It wasn't as if they were involved in a real relationship. She'd almost *pushed* him into making love.

"How are you doing?" Jase asked. "Really."

"Depends on when you ask me," she replied flippantly. "One minute I'm handling everything okay, the next . . ."

"I wanted to call you yesterday, but I thought you might need some space. The other night you said I 'nudged' you. I don't want to be pushy."

She smiled despite herself and shook her head. "It was a mutual decision, if I remember." Lord, did she remember. A change of subject was in order. "You're serious about not being able to do the surgery yourself?" she asked, just to be sure. If there was even a slight chance . . .

"Absolutely. It's simply not ethical. I'm sorry, Millie." He looked away, not meeting her gaze. There was something else, something he wasn't telling her.

"You and Dr. Daas aren't keeping anything from me, are you?" she asked cautiously.

His head swiveled sharply to meet her gaze.

"No, of course not. We've been totally up front with you about everything to do with Mary Jane."

"Okay. Sorry. Maybe I'm being paranoid, but I thought . . . I got the feeling you were holding something back just now."

He walked over to her chair and looked down at her, so close she could feel the familiar warmth of his body. "We've told you everything we know and everything we can guess about Mary Jane's condition and prognosis. I give you my word."

That was good enough for Millicent. She was out of the chair and into his arms before she knew it. He didn't hesitate but squeezed her tightly against him.

He didn't smell like a doctor should, she thought idly. Not like peppermint and alcohol, the way her pediatrician had smelled when she was a child. Jase's scent was much earthier, much more provocative.

"You can cry on my shoulder if you want, Millie."

She gave a little huff of a laugh. "No, I don't believe I will. I've done enough of that, thank you very much. And since when did you start calling me Millie?"

"Don't some of your friends and your family call you that?"

"Yes, but it sounds so intimate when you say it."

"If you don't like it—"

"No, I like it." She fingered the starched collar of his shirt, the soft, dark curls at the back of his neck. She was ashamed at how much she needed him, how essential he'd become to her in such a short time. A few weeks before she never would have dreamed she could feel this way about any man ever again.

After a few moments of letting him comfort her, she pulled away, embarrassed. He let her go, but he continued to stroke her hair, smoothing the stray strands that had escaped from her careless upsweep.

"I don't want it to be like this," she said, her voice shaking.

"None of us wants a child to be sick," Jase began, but she halted him with a raised hand.

"I wasn't talking about that. I mean you and me. I don't like it that I'm so . . . so desperate, and you're so giving. I like being with you, Jase. But if we're going to . . . I mean, I don't want you to feel obliged or anything. I'm a little emotional right now, but that doesn't mean I'll fall apart if you . . . well, if you should decide . . ." The words escaped her.

"You don't want me to feel sorry for you?" He sounded amazed. "Is that what you're trying to say?"

"Oh, I don't mind some sympathy." She sank back into her chair. Her legs didn't seem capable of supporting her anymore. "I just don't want that to be the only reason you . . . spend time with me. Because you think you can't abandon me—"

"I really had no intention of abandoning you. Let's get something clear. You're not some pathetic waif I've taken pity on. You're a beautiful, intelligent, exciting woman that I'm very, very attracted to." He pulled her out of the chair, and in one deft movement he sat down and swung her into his lap. "Do you find that so hard to believe?"

"Well . . . in a word, yes. It's like having the captain of the football team ask me to the prom—almost a laughable possibility."

"I'm not laughing." He swiveled her around and kissed her. She responded as naturally as if they'd been lovers for years. His touch was both familiar and excitingly new.

She could have easily gotten carried away right there in her pediatrician's office. But she kept her wits about her. She wasn't sure she'd made her point.

"Jase," she said, breathing hard.

"Yes?"

She leaned her head on his shoulder. It was easier to talk when she wasn't looking at him. "You know that, if not for the peculiar circumstances, I wouldn't have made love with you the other night."

"Yes, I understand that. But I think what *you* don't understand is, even without the peculiar circumstances, I wanted to make love to you. If you feel we've made a mistake, I can live with that. I can wait. I will wait. As long as it takes."

His apparent sincerity touched her. He really was something special. "I don't—" she began, then stopped herself. She didn't want to blow this by saying the wrong thing.

"C'mon, honey, what is it?"

She raised up and looked into those incredible velvety eyes. "I don't want to wait anymore. Life is too short and too unpredictable to worry about appearances and propriety and all that stupid stuff. I realized the other night that if I waited around for Ronnie to bless our relationship, I'd be waiting a very long time."

He grasped her chin and gently swiveled her head so that she was forced to look at him. He was smiling. "I'm glad you feel that way. Does that mean I can ask you out on another date?"

"Mmm, yes. Now. Tonight."

"Oh. I thought . . . tonight?"

"Hey, what is this? You refuse to do Mary Jane's surgery because you're involved with me. So be involved! If I'm going to pay the price, I might as well enjoy the benefits." She tried to sound playful, but his answer was really important to her. Were they involved, or merely "too close"?

He cleared his throat. "You won't hear any objections from this court. Tonight it is."

She nearly collapsed with relief.

"So, what about this evening?" he said briskly. "My kids are still up in Dallas, but we could take yours to a movie."

"My kids are at my mom and dad's house. I wanted them safely out of the way in case I needed to come home and fall apart after seeing Dr. Daas."

"And do you?"

She took a deep breath. "No. I've done all the

falling apart I want for now. I told Mom I'd pick up the kids around nine. We could hit the early show at the Majestic—"

He cut her off with another kiss, long and hot, then murmured, "Does the Majestic have a balcony where we can sit and make out?"

She wanted to chuckle at his audacity, but she couldn't quite summon that much humor. So she sighed. "It did, once. Then they chopped it up into three separate theaters, none of them with a balcony."

"Pity." He nuzzled her ear, his warm breath tickling.

"I heard the movie wasn't that good anyway."

His hand wandered to caress her breast. Her nipple tightened beneath the insistent graze of his thumb.

"I do believe you're trying to distract me, Dr. Desmond."

"Guilty as charged," he murmured, not the least bit chastened.

"You've been very good for me, you know," she said, her tone serious now. "When I'm with you, I feel more hopeful."

When she looked into his eyes, they seemed a little sad. "I'm glad," he said. Then he was kissing her again, passion rising like a hot tide, threatening to drown them both.

Millicent broke the kiss so that she could breathe. "Let's go home, huh?"

"Whose home?"

She thought about her house, with its toys and baby paraphernalia covering every square inch and the lunch dishes she hadn't quite gotten around to. And her bed, the one she'd shared with Ronnie.

She shook her head to clear it. Not that, not yet. "Yours. It's closer."

They went in separate cars. It was only a five-minute drive, but that was enough time for Millicent to think about what she was doing. They were going to Jase's house to have sex . . . make love, she amended. It sounded so tawdry, and yet it seemed so right. Was she just rationalizing her behavior? She and Ronnie had waited until they were married to consummate their love.

But she'd been a young girl then, innocent, idealistic. Circumstances were different now. She and Jase weren't contemplating marriage, but the bond between them was growing stronger every day.

Oh, hell, why didn't she just admit it? She needed Jase right now. Right or wrong, she needed him, and she wasn't about to deny herself. She was determined to get through her ordeal with Mary Jane any way she could.

Jase let Millicent in through the garage and into the kitchen. He stopped at the refrigerator to get them some white wine, then remembered what had happened last time they'd had wine, and opted for beer instead.

He never got the fridge open. Millicent was

right behind him, and when he turned to ask her preference, she was so close, he stopped mid-sentence.

He thought she was the most gorgeous creature he'd ever seen, and she didn't even recognize her own beauty. How had she gotten through twenty-nine years without anyone telling her how lovely she was? Delicate, fragile but strong, giving, caring. Her skin was as smooth and flawless as Mary Jane's, her hair like spun silk, her eyes as deep and rich as hot fudge.

They stood simply staring at each other for several heartbeats. Then he was kissing her again, and she was kissing him back with a hunger that matched his own. He'd never dreamed she could be so . . . *hot!*

"Upstairs?" he managed between kisses.

"Mm-hmm," she replied, but they never made it past the living room, where late afternoon sunlight shone through the floor-to-ceiling windows. Items of clothing fell one by one in a heap on the floor. Shoes were kicked across the room. Jase delighted in removing the pins from Millicent's hair, watching the golden-brown tresses sift down to her bare shoulders. Her eyes were smoky with desire, her naked breasts surging forward, the nipples full and hard.

Determined to take things slower this time, he eased her onto the puffy designer sofa that no one ever sat on. He knelt on the floor beside her and kissed her from her forehead down to her toes, pausing along the way for leisurely tours of her breasts and her sensitive inner thighs. She sighed at first, then moaned, then pleaded with him to put her out of her misery.

But he tortured her a little more. He'd never been with a woman more responsive to his touch. He was near to exploding with desire himself, but he held on, intent on pleasuring her. She'd given him a rare gift, and he wouldn't abuse it.

Her patience had its limits. All at once she sat up, fire and determination in her eyes, and swung her legs to the floor. "Sit by me," she commanded.

He didn't dare disobey her, not when she was looking at him as if she wanted to eat him alive. He levered himself up and sat down beside her, curious as to what she had in mind.

He didn't have to wait long. She moved to her knees, never taking her eyes off him. Then she straddled him, lowering herself onto his erection with torturous deliberation, slowly enveloping him in her velvet warmth.

"Millicent." Her name was a caress. Her consuming desire moved him. No one had ever wanted him this way, not Libby, not any of the other women. The way she gazed at him was a turn-on. The way the tip of her tongue toyed with her lower lip drove him to distraction.

With inhuman determination he kept himself in check, letting Millicent do as she would. She leaned forward, her ear against his, her hair tickling his shoulder and neck, her arms wrapped around him, and moved with a slow, sensual rhythm.

The pace accelerated, her breathing coming in quick gasps. One last kiss and then she closed her eyes, tensed, bit her lip. "Oh, oh. Oh!" She smiled as the climax overtook her.

With two quick, intense strokes Jase let go, and he could have sworn that their combined ecstasy shook the room.

When he opened his eyes, he felt dizzy with satisfaction. Millicent clung to him as if he were a lifesaver in the middle of a stormy ocean.

"What has gotten into me?" she asked, her voice full of wonder. "It's broad daylight, in your living room!"

Jase laughed, low and wicked. "I don't know, but I hope it sticks around."

"Maybe your daughter was right. Maybe I *am* a slut. I've never behaved this way in my life!"

"Then I guess it's about time, don't you?" When she didn't respond, he got serious, realizing she might truly be troubled by her own passionate nature. "You haven't done anything wrong. We have exceptional chemistry, that's all. We bring out the best in each other."

"Jase?"

"What?"

"We didn't use birth control. We must be out of our minds."

That gave him pause. The thought of going upstairs and finding a condom hadn't even crossed his mind. "I don't know what to say, except that when I'm kissing you, my brain short-circuits. I'm sorry."

"It's not your fault alone. I'm as much to blame. Maybe subconsciously I *want* another baby," she said forlornly. "I do love babies."

"We were carried away. Let's just leave it at that and try to do better next time, okay?" If there was a next time. Jase was beginning to wonder if he really was good for Millicent. He might bring her some momentary pleasure, but she couldn't hide those pangs of conscience.

Lord, what if they'd made a baby? The thought gave him a pleasurable tingle, followed by a truck-load of guilt.

Then there was Mary Jane. If not for his involvement with Millicent, he could do the surgery. He was damn good when it came to delicate operations. He could give that baby as good a chance as any surgeon in the state.

It wasn't just the ethics that prevented him from taking on Mary Jane. Technically he could do it. She wasn't a relative, and he was capable of divorcing himself from his emotions when he picked up a scalpel. But if he lost her—or if she ended up a quadriplegic—he wouldn't be able to face Millicent. He wouldn't be able to face himself.

Libby had put her life in his hands. He'd made promises he couldn't keep. He'd failed her, and she'd never forgiven him. He couldn't bear for that to happen with Millicent.

❖————❖

Saturday morning. Millicent had picked up the kids at her parents' house the night before, never mentioning Jase, never mentioning her visit with Dr. Daas. She was jumpy as a cat, but if the children noticed, they didn't say anything.

This morning she was trying to work off some excess tension at her potter's wheel. This was her third attempt. Mary Jane lay in her mesh playpen a few feet away. She seemed to like the whine and groan of the wheel.

"Mom, is something wrong?"

Millicent jumped. The clay vessel she'd been forming turned into a formless lump. "Oh, hi, Nancy." Yes, something was terribly wrong. Her baby was sick. But she hadn't decided exactly what to tell the other kids. She believed in being honest with her children to a point, but she didn't want to traumatize them.

She hit the foot pedal on the wheel and watched it slowly decelerate. The wet clay went back into the plastic bag with a plop. "Guess I'm not feeling all that creative right now. Anyway, I wasn't doing very well with this bandaged hand." She wrinkled her nose at the strips of gauze, which were now filthy. Maybe she could get Jase to change the bandage. . . .

"Did you practice your viola today?" she asked as she wiped her hands with a wet cloth.

"You answer my question first. You've been acting really funny, and I know something's wrong."

Perceptive little minx, Millicent thought.

"What did you do yesterday after you shuffled us off to Grandma and Granddad's? Hot date with Dr. Desmond?" she asked smugly.

"For your information, smarty-pants, I went to see Dr. Daas."

"Our Dr. Daas?" Nancy already looked stricken, and she didn't even know what was wrong. "Why?"

"Mary Jane is sick," Millicent blurted out. It felt good to get it off her chest, even though she knew Nancy would be crushed. The girl adored her baby sister.

"Sick how?" Nancy's eyes filled with tears. "Oh my God. I'm sorry about that crack I made about Dr. Desmond. I had no idea—"

"It's okay, honey." Millicent patted her daughter's shoulder.

"What's wrong with Mary Jane?"

Millicent explained things as clearly as she could, as honestly as she could. It wouldn't be fair to sugar-coat the bad news. If the worst happened, she wanted the other kids to be prepared.

Nancy was a bright girl, and she had no trouble grasping the situation. "She could die, couldn't she?"

Millicent swallowed the lump in her throat. "It's a small possibility."

"When will it happen?"

"As soon as I can get the surgery scheduled. Within a couple of weeks, I imagine."

Nancy went to the playpen and picked Mary Jane up, supporting her head as Millicent had taught her. The baby, oblivious, caught a piece of Nancy's hair and pulled delightedly.

Nancy hardly seemed to feel it. "Is that why you've been spending time with Dr. Desmond?"

"Partly. He's been a great source of strength and comfort for me. But that's not the only reason."

"Are you in love with him?"

Millicent gazed miserably at her daughter. "I'm afraid it's looking that way."

"Will you get married?" The question was neutral—not hopeful, but at least it wasn't filled with dread.

"I don't know. I'm not sure he feels the same. Anyway, I'm not willing to make you and the other kids miserable just to make myself happy. If you really don't want him around, then I won't bring him around." And so much for not allowing Nancy and Will to dictate to her.

Her kids came first. That was how it had to be.

"I don't know how I feel anymore," Nancy said. Then she gave a sad little chuckle. "If you and Dr. Desmond got married, Valerie would be my sister. She would freak."

"And you wouldn't?"

Nancy thought about it. "I wouldn't have to share my room, would I?"

Millicent laughed too. "I don't know. But let's

not worry about that now. First we have to get Mary Jane through her surgery."

Hugging the baby to her, Nancy let a small tear escape down her cheek. "Yeah. We better tell Will. And Lily, even though she won't understand."

Millicent was on her third surgeon. The first one, out of Tyler, had seemed very nice. He'd spent a long time on the phone with her, patiently answering her anxious questions, not bothered in the least by her interrogation about his experience. She'd had a bit of a communication problem with the second one because of his strong Middle Eastern accent. But she'd persisted, and his credentials had impressed her. Now she was talking to Dr. Boynton, the one with whom Jase had interned. She was favorably inclined toward him on that qualification alone.

"Where did you say you lived again?" Dr. Boynton asked.

"Near Destiny."

"Say, you know, you've got one of the best neurosurgeons in the state right in your backyard. I hope he's on your list of candidates. Jase Desmond?"

Millicent's breath caught in her throat. This made three out of three who'd mentioned Jase and heartily recommended him. "Yes, I know Dr. Desmond. I understand he interned with you."

Dr. Boynton laughed. "More like I interned

with him. He was always up on the latest procedures. When he wasn't working with a patient, he
had his nose stuck in some medical journal or he
was jetting off someplace to observe a tricky surgery. One of the best young doctors I ever had the
privilege to work with. Gifted, really. You couldn't
go wrong with him."

Oh, couldn't I? she wondered.

"Of course, I'll be happy to take on your little
one," Dr. Boynton continued. "We have all the latest technology here at Parkland, and I've done
many, many surgeries of this type—though mostly
on adults. But I hope you'll give Dr. Desmond due
consideration. He's young yet, but he's . . . well,
the best."

"I see. Thank you so much for your candor, Dr.
Boynton. I'll be making a decision quickly, and I'll
get back to you."

"Good, good. My best to you and your family,
whatever you decide."

Millicent hung up the phone, her heart pound-
ing. The best. They all said he was the best, dammit. And there was nothing in the world that would
prevent her from getting the best for her baby. She
knew what she had to do.

Her hand shaking, she reached for the phone
and dialed Jase's number at the hospital.

EIGHT

Jase was working Emergency again, examining a twelve-year-old girl who'd gone through the windshield of her mother's truck, when his beeper went off. Damn. The switchboard knew not to beep him when he was in the E.R. Unless it was a personal emergency . . .

He thought first of his own kids, then about Mary Jane. Had the baby experienced some sort of medical crisis? Had they delayed the surgery too long?

His current patient was dazed but not critical. With a reassuring smile, he sent the little girl to X-ray, then found a phone. "Desmond here. You beeped me?"

"Yes. Millicent Jones called. She said it was important but not an emergency. But she sounded rather agitated, so I thought I'd better let you know."

"Okay, thanks. I've got the number." He almost dreaded calling her. Not because he didn't want to hear her voice, but because he'd been doing a lot of thinking over the weekend. He knew what he had to do. But it was going to come near to killing him to do it. He dialed her number.

"Millicent? It's Jase."

"Oh, Jase. Thanks for returning my call so quickly. I know I must have sounded like a crazy woman to your switchboard operator—"

"Is something wrong?"

"No. Well, yes. I need to see you as soon as possible. In person."

"That sounds a little ominous," Jase said with a levity he didn't feel.

"It's important."

He swallowed, trying to ease his suddenly dry mouth. "I'll be off at three o'clock. Shall I meet you for coffee?"

"No, I don't have a sitter. I was hoping you could come here."

"Sure. Truth is, I need to talk to you too."

"Oh? Now, *that* sounds ominous . . ."

He didn't give her any reassurances. "I'll be at your place around three-thirty."

"I'll put on some coffee." They hung up.

Jase could hardly make it through the rest of his shift for worrying about the confrontation to come. Thankfully, his patient had noting more than a mild concussion and some cuts and abrasions. He admitted her overnight for observation.

He wasn't so lucky with his next patient. An elderly woman arrived by ambulance complaining of chest pains. Jase had no more than gotten her settled into an examining room when she went into cardiac arrest.

He grabbed the phone and punched the intercom button. "I have a Code Blue in exam room four," he said. "I need a crash cart and every free hand."

In seconds he had another doctor and three more nurses with him. They worked on the woman for almost an hour. But finally they were forced to abandon their efforts. Her frail body had given up.

With a start, Jase realized he recognized her. She'd been a volunteer at the Y where Valerie had taken swimming lessons a couple of years before. It was weird how he hadn't really looked at her, at her face, until the crisis was over.

Now came the hard part. Jase had to break the news to the woman's husband that she hadn't made it.

The old man broke down crying, and Jase was at a loss. "We gave it our best shot," he said, touching the man's trembling shoulder.

The man jerked away from Jase's hand. "Your best shot wasn't good enough, was it?" he said belligerently through his tears. Then he shot out of the consultation room before Jase could stop him, moving much faster than a man his age ought to be able to.

Jase sighed. The old man's words rang in his head, over and over.

Three o'clock couldn't have come soon enough, yet Jase found himself dragging his feet when his shift was finally over. He changed into jeans and a fresh shirt he kept in his office, gave his face a slap-dash shave with an electric razor, and combed his hair. When he couldn't procrastinate any longer, he headed out.

During the drive to Millicent's home, beads of perspiration formed on his forehead and upper lip, even though the air conditioner in his car was on at full blast. His stomach was in knots. Too much cof-fee, he told himself. He should have asked Millie to make decaf.

Millie. How had he come to care for her so deeply, so quickly? It had started with the bond they'd formed when he'd delivered her baby. But even without that, he knew he would have been drawn to her like a cat to curtain fringe. She was utterly irresistible to him. The essence of wom-anhood. His own Venus in Blue Jeans, like the old song.

Only not his own for very long.

She greeted him at the door with a wary smile. Wearing denim shorts and a short, peach-colored top that revealed a strip of creamy skin at her waist, she'd never looked more beautiful to him. He hadn't really noticed until now that she'd been losing her postpartum weight. Her tummy was flat, her waist nipped in, and a rib or two showed.

They busied themselves with small talk and coffee. The baby sat in her chair on the kitchen table, and Jase studied her for any signs of deterioration, but she looked the same. She smiled delightedly at him as she always did. He looked away, closing off his heart.

Lily, who was gradually warming up to him, brought him a picture book and stared up at him beseechingly.

"What do you have there, punkin?" Jase asked, giving Millicent a help-me-out-here look. Now was not the time to be insinuating himself any further into her family.

Millicent seemed to read his dilemma perfectly, although how could she know? "Oh, no you don't," she said, scooping Lily into her arms. She looked over the little girl's shoulder at Jase. "She knows it's about nap time, and she'll look for any distraction to postpone it."

At the word "nap," Lily issued an unladylike shriek.

"Oh, dear." Millicent rolled her eyes. "I'll put the girls down and be back in a minute."

Jase resisted the urge to go with her as she carried the baby and led a sobbing Lily to the back of the house, where the bedrooms were. Those kids sure knew how to wedge their way into a guy's heart.

So did their mama.

She returned in a few minutes, rolling her eyes. "What a production."

"Ginger cries when she goes down too," he commiserated.

"I let Lily sleep in the baby's crib along with Mary Jane. She goes down easier if she can nap with her little sister."

"I can remember doing the same thing with Heather and Ginger. Sometimes I'd do anything to keep them from crying. I'm a soft touch."

"Yeah, me too." She refreshed his coffee. "So, what did you want to talk about?"

"You first." He wasn't at all sure how he wanted to broach the decision he'd made.

"Okay. I interviewed all the surgeons today."

Jase relaxed a bit. Sounded like all she wanted was someone to help her make the final choice. "And?"

"All three of them recommended you."

He tensed again. "Uh-huh."

"I want the best for Mary Jane. You're the best. It's that simple."

It wasn't simple at all. He sighed wearily, wondering where to go from there. Was he sure? Very sure? Instead of responding to her ultimatum, he changed the subject. "I lost a patient in the E.R. today."

Her face fell. "Oh, Jase, I'm so sorry. And here I am, nagging you. What happened?"

"An elderly woman. Her heart." He wasn't sure why he was telling Millicent this. Losing patients was part of being a doctor. The worst part, to be sure, but it happened from time to time. "I knew her, vaguely."

"Oh, how awful. I'm sure that makes it much harder. I'm also sure you did everything you could."

He nodded. *Your best shot wasn't good enough, was it?*

She wrapped her small, delicate artist's hand around his larger one. Her grip was surprisingly strong. "You know, I have complete faith in you."

"Please don't say that. I'm not a miracle worker."

"Only God is a miracle worker. Truth be known, I'm counting on Him too."

"Nice to know I'm in good company."

"Does that mean you'll do it?"

This was his last chance to back out. "I don't want to. I don't want the responsibility. But . . ."

She continued to look at him with the same beseeching expression Lily had used on him a few minutes ago. He tried, but he couldn't harden his heart to her.

"You're not giving me much choice," he said.

"It might not be nice of me, but I didn't intend to give you a choice." She looked down into her lap. "I know I'm risking a lot by backing you into a corner. But I have to. I don't have a choice, either."

Jase took a long sip of his coffee. As if he needed more caffeine. "I'm not being entirely fair to you here, putting the burden of this decision all on you.

Actually I've been thinking about it all day—about offering to do the surgery."

She looked up, hopeful. "Really?"

"Yeah. But there's something you have to understand. If I'm to be Mary Jane's surgeon . . ." He paused, practically wrenching his next few words from his gut. ". . . then I'll have nothing more to do with you or your family except on a strictly professional basis."

She looked down again. Her soft brown hair fell forward, shadowing her face. But Jase could still see the anguish there. He hated like hell that he was the source of any more pain.

"I guess I can't blame you for wanting to be ethical," she said in a small voice.

"It's not just ethics." How could he make her understand? "Emotional involvement and medicine don't mix. A doctor has to be completely detached to do his best work in the operating room. His or her concentration has to be one hundred percent on the job at hand. Sentiment, fear, doubts—if any of those creep in, the concentration can falter, the hand can shake—"

"I'm getting the picture," she said with a slight shiver. When she spoke again, her tone was brisk, businesslike. "So, we'll just stop seeing each other, then. We're not so deep into this thing that we can't back out. I wasn't ready to get involved with anyone, anyway." Her words were offhand, but Jase wasn't fooled. It hurt her as much to say them as it did him to hear them.

"Right. Maybe it's for the best. But if you want to change your mind—"

"No," she said with a gritty determination that he couldn't help but admire. "I'd be incredibly, disgustingly selfish to put my love life ahead of my daughter's welfare. You're the one to remove that tumor."

"Then I'll do it." He forced himself into his professional mode. "I'll schedule the surgery for next week. Is Thursday a good day?"

"As good as any," she said in a monotone, still staring at the floor.

"I'll let you know." He stood abruptly and took his empty cup to the sink, studiously avoiding Millicent's gaze. If he looked at her again, his resolve would crumble. He felt the urge to kiss her, to hold her one last time, but he knew if he did, he'd never be able to walk away.

Somehow he managed to get out the door.

Millicent didn't cry. She had no more tears left inside her. Anyway, she'd suspected what his reaction would be before he'd responded to her request. She'd been prepared for him to break things off—as prepared as any woman can be for that sort of thing.

Jase had agreed to do the surgery. That was what mattered. First thing tomorrow morning she would have to call the other three surgeons and tell them of the decision she'd made. Right now, though, she had a more unpleasant task. She had to tell Will and Lily about their baby sister's illness. She woke Lily from her nap, leaving Mary Jane sleeping peacefully in her crib. Then she called the other two kids into the living room and sat them all down on the sofa.

Nancy already knew, of course. She simply sat there, biting her nails, saying nothing.

Will took the news the hardest. He was only eight, but he understood death all too well since his father's passing. Millicent could tell he was terrified at the prospect of losing the baby sister he'd so recently come to love. Even Lily started crying, understanding only that something bad was happening.

She gathered them all to her, squeezing between Will and Nancy, pulling Lily into her lap. They sat that way for a long time, soaking up strength from each other.

"Tell you what," Millicent said when the tears had slowed to a trickle. "Let's all of us do something as a family tomorrow. I know. We'll go to the county fair over in Crumley."

"That's a good idea," Nancy said, putting on a cheerful mien for the other kids' benefit. "We can go on the pony rides. I bet Lily's never ridden a pony before."

"Pony?" Lily said. "Like My Little Ponies?"

"Or maybe a horsey," Will clarified for her. "Like Mr. Ed."

"Can we ride the horsey, Mama?"

"Sure we can. I've even been thinking we might

buy our own horse. It would be great exercise, and it would be good for you kids to be responsible for a pet."

"That'd be cool," Will said.

Nancy's face crumpled. "I've always wanted a pony," she said. "But if I had one, I'd gladly give it back if it would make Mary Jane all right."

"I know, sweetie," Millicent said, hugging Nancy again. "We're all pulling for her."

"I s'pose Dr. Desmond will want to go with us to the fair?" Nancy asked.

"No," Millicent replied, a little more sharply than she'd intended. She softened her tone. "As a matter of fact, Dr. Desmond and I won't be seeing each other anymore, unless it has something to do with Mary Jane's surgery." She tried her best to sound unconcerned, but it had to be the biggest acting job she'd ever done. "You kids were right. It really wasn't time for me to be dating again. Maybe someday, but right now we need to pull together. Just us Joneses."

Will and Nancy exchanged a look that Millicent couldn't interpret.

She glanced at her watch. "Goodness, look at the time. I've got to get dinner started, and Nancy, you need to get your viola practicing in. Or, if you kids want, you can go out to the barn and see how good a shape it's in. Make a list of things we need to do to get ready for a horse."

The children brightened a bit at this suggestion. "Get a notebook and pen, Will," Nancy said. "I'll find that book on horses we got for Christmas last year."

The older kids shot off with Lily tagging behind. Millicent smiled. She'd distracted them, at least for a while. Maybe she was crazy to be thinking about buying a horse, but the preparations would keep everyone's minds occupied. She knew from experience that pain was more bearable if you just kept moving.

Jase got through the next few days by concentrating on the job at hand. He read every article on spinal tumors that he could find on the Internet and an on-line medical library, as well as the medical library at Stockton University. He ordered more tests for his tiny patient. He threw himself into his work with the zeal he'd shown studying for his med school entrance exam. And when he wasn't focusing on Mary Jane Jones's case, he was immersing himself in other work.

He resisted the urge to volunteer for extra shifts at the hospital, because he wanted to be well rested for the tricky surgery to come. But when he got home each day, he didn't rest or unwind. He did yard work, cleaned out the garage, painted the exterior trim, washed his car.

He was grateful when the kids returned from their visit with their grandparents, because it gave him more things to do. He took them places, bought them things, played games with them. And, thank goodness, they didn't ask him any curious questions about Millicent Jones.

Millie. He tried desperately not to think about her. By keeping so busy, sometimes he managed to banish her from his mind for minutes at a time.

Nights were the worst. When he wasn't visualizing her in his bed, he was dreaming about her. Sometimes the dreams were pleasant fantasies, from which he would wake up with a keen sense of disappointment that the dream wasn't real, then a longing in his gut so sharp, it produced physical pain.

Sometimes the dreams were unpleasant—like the one where he went to her house and found it empty, the whole family having mysteriously vanished. And worse—he dreamed that he was starting Mary Jane's surgery, but suddenly he couldn't remember what to do. He would look at her tiny form on the sterile-draped table, as if viewing her through a film of Vaseline, and his mind would go blank.

He woke up from that dream in a cold sweat, breathing as if he'd just run a marathon and thanking the heavens that it wasn't real. He'd never frozen up in an operating room, and he didn't intend to start now.

Still, the next day he took the added precaution of calling in his former colleague and mentor, Rick Boynton, to assist with the delicate operation. If Millicent's insurance company didn't like it, he'd pay the doctor's hefty fee out of his own pocket.

By early the following week, even though he was hideously distracted, he noticed something peculiar happening with his two older girls. There was a lot of whispering going on, a lot of secretive phone calls that ended with a furtively muttered "I'll have to call you back."

When the third such phone call came during dinner one night, Jase couldn't contain his curiosity any longer. "All right, Val, who's been calling?"

"Um, no one. Just a friend from school."

"A friend, huh? Might this friend be a boy?"

Valerie looked down, suddenly interested in her pork chop. Then her gaze shot up. "Uh, yeah, that's it, Dad. Can't fool you, I guess."

Oh, great. Valerie was only ten, and boy crazy already? "Look, Val, I don't mind if you want to talk on the phone to boys, but ask them not to call during our dinner hour, please, and I don't want you on the phone twenty-four hours a day."

"Okay." She acquiesced so easily that Jase's suspicions intensified.

"Is there one boy in particular that you like better than the others?"

"Yeah," Heather piped in. "His name is Nan—Neil."

"Shut up, Heather," Valerie said.

"Val, I don't want you talking to your sister that way. You don't have to tell me about this boy if you don't want to. I just thought you might want to."

"I don't," she said a little desperately. "Dad, can I be excused?"

"Sure, hon." Inwardly Jase winced. He'd suspected his daughter was growing up too fast; now he was positive. He would have to spend the next ten years guarding her virtue with his life.

Heather popped out of her chair the same instant Valerie did. They rinsed their plates in the sink, then scurried out of the kitchen and upstairs—to use the phone, no doubt.

The next afternoon his girls were behaving even more strangely. "Dad, will you take me and Heather to Nick's Pizza Palace tonight?" Valerie asked in her best wheedling tone.

"And not Ginger?"

"Ginger doesn't like pizza anyway. Besides, it's been a long time since we had you to ourselves. Just us big girls."

Jase shrugged. "Well, if it's all right with Saundra." He didn't know whether to be flattered by the request or wary, but curiosity was getting the better of him. He had a sneaking suspicion this Neil character might be showing up at the pizza parlor, and Jase wanted a good look at the kid.

"Hurry, Dad," Heather said as he backed the car out of the garage. "We have to be there by six-thirty."

"Oh, really?" he commented. "I didn't realize we were on a tight schedule."

"It's just that it gets crowded later on," Valerie said, sending a murderous glare toward the backseat. "When it's crowded, all the best slices on the buffet disappear."

"Ah." Sure. As if Valerie ate anything except plain cheese pizza anyway. "Are you sure you want to do Nick's?" he asked, enjoying the look of panic his words brought to Val's face. She'd chosen the noisy family pizza joint for a reason. "You complained about it last time we went. We could try that new Italian place over on—"

"No," both girls objected together.

"Heather really likes Nick's," Val said, as if she always thought of her sister's welfare above her own. "And I heard they have a new video game that's really cool."

"Uh-huh. What's it called?"

"Alien Warriors," Valerie said, at the exact same time Heather shouted out, "Mutant Lizards."

"Alien Warriors has mutant lizards in it, Bozo," Valerie said. Another murderous glare.

Jase chuckled inwardly. He was glad to know his daughters were rotten liars. Might come in handy when they really were teenagers.

The restaurant crowd was light. Jase ordered and paid for their dinners, then took his tray through the buffet line and mindlessly filled his plate with pizza. Remembering his resolution to be exceptionally healthy this week, he got a salad too. His daughters made their usual picky-eater choices, then dragged Jase to a big table that would easily seat eight.

"Why don't we move to a smaller table," Jase

tried to suggest, but the girls were already sitting down, their eyes glued to a show on the big-screen TV. With a sigh he joined them.

"Dad, can we each have a dollar for the video games?" Valerie asked, her eyes darting around the room furtively. "You can take it out of next week's allowance."

"Sure, I guess." He pulled out his wallet and handed each girl a single. They clutched the bills, but made no move to retire to the game room. They kept staring at the door.

It would be a shame if Valerie's puppy love interest stood her up, Jase caught himself thinking. He remembered the agonies of adolescent crushes. They weren't nearly as harrowing as the adult relationships he'd weathered, but bad enough.

Nothing could match the torture he'd put himself through with Millicent. Maybe, if the surgery went well, if Mary Jane made a full recovery, if . . . No. He wouldn't let his hopes wander in that direction. What could he do, tell Millicent, "Sure, I want to be with you, but only if you have a perfectly normal baby?" Love didn't work that way. You had to take the good with the bad. When the bad he anticipated was so terrible he didn't think he could stand it, he had to bail out.

"There she is," Heather hissed, then clamped her hand over her mouth. She was treated to murderous glare number three.

"C'mon, Heather," Valerie said through gritted teeth, dragging her sister out of her chair. "Let's go check out Alien Warriors." They bolted from the table.

"There *she* is?" Jase repeated to empty air. Then, in one clarifying moment, he understood what this whole drama was about. Millicent Jones had just walked through the front door of Nick's.

NINE

"I really don't see why it matters if we're late," Millicent said as Will and Nancy dragged her through the door of Nick's Pizza Palace. "I don't even know why we came here. I had a perfectly good meat loaf ready to put in the oven—"

"We haven't been here in ages," Nancy said. "Besides, we thought it would be nice if you didn't have to cook dinner for a change."

"But I like to cook! Have I ever complained?" That was one of the benefits of being a domestic goddess, she'd always told Callie and Lana. She had the time to plan meals, clip recipes, try new things. Cooking kept her hands busy. Kept her from throwing things or pulling her hair out.

Mary Jane's surgery was in two days.

She supposed she shouldn't begrudge the kids a pizza night. They'd been extraordinary since her talk with them the previous week—doing their chores, never complaining, never fighting. It was as if they knew any small incident could drive their mother over the edge.

"One adult buffet, two children's, two drinks, one water, please," Millicent said to the cashier.

"Hey, Mom," Nancy said, "you won't believe who's here. Dr. Desmond."

Millicent snapped to attention, her hand automatically going to smooth her flyaway hair. Jase, here? Since their dismal conversation in her kitchen, she'd avoided any face-to-face contact with him, even during those frightening, never-ending medical tests. He communicated with her through a secretary or nurse.

She looked awful! Not that it mattered, she scolded herself. Jase didn't care what she looked like, not anymore.

"Aren't you at least going to say hi?" Nancy asked. "I know y'all aren't dating anymore, but you don't have to be rude."

"Oh, excuse me?" Millicent said, smelling a rat. Now her kids' recent clandestine behavior was making sense. "Aren't you the one who went up a tree with a book to avoid talking to Valerie Desmond?"

"And aren't you the one who pointed out that it was rude?" Nancy countered with a smug smile. Before Millicent could object, her son and daughter made a beeline for the Desmonds' table. At least, she assumed he was there with his kids, although he sat alone. She didn't imagine Nick's was the sort of restaurant he would choose for himself.

It seemed she had no choice but to follow her sneaky offspring. Jase was looking right at her. There was no way to avoid at least saying hi. If the rueful expression on Jase's face was any indication, he'd been similarly hoodwinked by his children.

"Hello, Jase. Fancy meeting you here," she said as casually as she dared, taking a chair a safe distance from him. She could do this. She could.

Jase gave Millicent's children a hard stare as they gobbled down pizza. They studiously avoided acknowledging him. "If I gave them each a buck," Jase said in a loud stage whisper, "do you think they'd go away and play video games?"

"I already gave them money," Millicent said. Before the words were even out of her mouth, Nancy and Will had each grabbed a wedge of pizza and fled from the table. "Hmm. I hope you don't think I had anything to do—"

Jase held up his hand. "Say no more. It wasn't my idea, either. I'm going to ground those kids till they're old enough to vote."

"I'm putting mine on bread and water," Millicent agreed glumly. She mashed her pizza around with a fork, having lost her appetite.

"You doing okay?" Jase asked, his voice warm with concern. It was the concern that undid her. If he'd only remain impersonal, the way he'd been the other day, she could handle this untenable situation much better.

"Fine," she answered tightly, holding herself together by sheer willpower. "You?"

"Fine."

Millicent forced herself to eat pizza. The sooner she finished, the sooner she could reasonably leave without revealing how much his nearness affected her. A small part of her wanted to hurt him for rejecting her when she'd gone out so far on a limb to give him what he'd asked of her—when he'd been actively pursuing her. But another part of her—the mom in her—wanted Jase in tip-top form when he performed his surgery on Mary Jane. She didn't want him thinking about her, or feeling guilty, or second-guessing himself when his attention should be on his patient.

"Millicent," he began, but she wouldn't allow it.

"You don't have to say anything. You've made your feelings abundantly clear. The kids obviously thought they were doing the right thing by throwing us together. So let's just finish eating and leave, all right?"

He slumped down in his chair, looking defeated. "Yeah. You're right, of course."

As she chewed and swallowed the suddenly dry pizza, she sneaked covert glances at Jase. Just as she feared. He was as sexy as she remembered. Her memories hadn't been exaggerated. He'd finally gotten that haircut, but he still looked dangerous to her.

Dangerous to her heart, that was for sure.

Without warning, a piece of pizza crust lodged in her throat. She choked, sputtered, coughed, drank some water.

"Millicent, are you all right?" He was around the table in an instant and standing behind her chair, his hands on her shoulder. For heaven's sake, she was trying to breathe. By touching her, he wasn't helping any.

"I'm . . . okay," she managed between coughing spasms.

"Sure?" He leaned around her and peered into her face. The expression of anxiety he wore was more than the standard doctor's concern.

She nodded emphatically, thankful that the tears filling her eyes could be blamed on the strangling. After a few more coughs and some more water, she recovered enough so that she could at least talk. "I'm okay now. For a minute there I thought you were going to have to do the Heimlich maneuver on me."

A picture flashed briefly in her mind of Jase with his arms around her. . . . Oh, no. She banished the image to that locked compartment in her mind where all such memories were languishing.

Perhaps the same thought had flashed through Jase's mind, because he squeezed her shoulders briefly, then touched her hair before seeming to remember himself.

He backed away, retreated to his side of the table.

This was ridiculous. She was going to embarrass herself further if she didn't get out of there. She pushed her almost untouched plate away. "Guess

I'm out of here. I'll—will I see you Thursday morning?" Slippery territory here.

"Probably not," he said, stirring his watery soft drink with his straw. "I'll be very busy before the surgery, making preparations, going over the game plan with Dr. Boynton, going over last-minute test results—"

"Yes, of course. I understand."

"You'll be kept constantly informed—"

"I know. I just want to say that I know you'll do the best job possible. Whatever the outcome—"

"She'll come through fine," Jase said with grim determination, as if by merely willing it, he could make it so.

He was trying to bolster her spirits, she realized. It was the first time he'd said anything even remotely optimistic. Which was why she didn't take any real comfort from his words. It was just one of those platitudes people mouth when they didn't know what else to say. She'd heard so many of the same reassurances after Ronnie had been rushed to the hospital by ambulance. Later she'd learned that he'd already been dead by the time they had loaded him onto the stretcher.

She had to say something, anything, that would let Jase off the hook. "I'm hoping for the best, of course," she said. "But if the worst hap—" Her voice caught. She cleared her throat and tried again. "If the worst happens, I will survive it. I survived my husband's death. I've also lost a brother and a sister. Life goes on. It seems as if it won't, for a while, but then it does." The words seemed harsh, but she sensed it was what he needed to hear. He literally held her baby's life in his hands, but she couldn't allow him to feel solely responsible for the ultimate outcome.

He cleared his throat. His eyes were just a little shinier than normal.

"I guess you knew that," she continued. "But I wanted to make sure you knew *I* understood it. Please don't worry about me."

"I can't really help that," he said. He looked completely miserable.

She couldn't think of anything else to ease his mind. Well, no matter. She had to believe that, when the time came, he would prove himself the consummate professional and push all personal thoughts aside. With a final nod in his direction, she stood, grabbed her purse, and headed for the video game room.

When she got to the crowded room, which hummed and beeped and throbbed with a life all its own, it took her a few moments to locate her children. They were in a far corner, huddled in conference with two other little girls . . . Jase's girls? Valerie and Nancy were in here together and no bones were broken?

"Nancy!" Millicent called out.

Nancy's head snapped up. The expression on her face was pure guilt.

"Hello, Valerie, Heather," Millicent said pleasantly, not giving anyone a hint of her inner turmoil.

"Nice to see you again. Kids?" She addressed her own two. "We're leaving."

"But, Mom, we still—"

"We're leaving," she said again. "Now."

Nancy and Will hung their heads like a couple of scolded puppies and trudged out of the game room. Millicent herded them in front of her to ensure they didn't try to make any detours by Jase's table. They'd done enough harm with their interference.

Nothing more was said until they were all in the car. Then Millicent's anger got the best of her. "Well, that was a load of laughs."

"I guess it didn't work, then," Will said glumly from the backseat.

"Darn straight it didn't," Millicent retorted. "The only thing you succeeded with was to embarrass your mother half to death and make Dr. Desmond feel very uncomfortable. It's not a good idea to meddle with other people's lives, particularly when strong feelings are involved. Did you think this was like some Saturday night sitcom, where people scheme and lie and have silly misunderstandings and pull all kinds of crazy stunts, but everything works out in the end? Because real life isn't like that. Dr. Desmond and I didn't have some kind of spat or lover's quarrel. We decided, for some very good reasons, to end our relationship. Now because of your thoughtless meddling . . . well, you just don't know the harm you might have done."

Nancy mumbled something unintelligible.

"What? I didn't hear you."

"It wasn't thoughtless," she said carefully, deliberately. "When you told me you and Dr. Desmond had broken things off, I knew it was because of us, because Valerie and Heather and me and Will didn't want y'all dating. You even told me that, that if we didn't want Dr. Desmond around, you'd stop seeing him."

Millicent did recall saying something like that.

"So that's why you broke up, right? I was happy about it at first, but then I saw how sad you were, almost as bad as when Daddy died, and I knew I had to do something. It was my fault, and I had to fix it. Valerie and I talked a long time about what to do. We thought that if we showed you that we could all get along and that we didn't mind—" A sob interrupted the flow of words.

Hearing Nancy's anguish softened Millicent. She had no call to strike out at her children just because she was in pain. "Listen to me, please. Jase breaking things off with me had nothing to do with you kids. Really."

"Then what was it?" Will asked.

"Something I couldn't explain if I wanted to."

"Did we really harm anyone?" Nancy asked, sincerely concerned. "Remember, you said we didn't realize the harm we might have done."

Millicent was ashamed to realize that, in the midst of her own emotional crisis, she'd almost said something about the foolhardiness of messing with Jase's mind when he would be removing Mary

Jane's tumor in thirty-six hours. How could she be so careless? She might have saddled her children with guilt that would last a lifetime.

She opened the car window to get some fresh air, even though it was still stiflingly hot outside. "I was exaggerating," she said. "I'm sorry I flew off the handle. No real harm was done, and I know you meant well. But let me and Jase handle this thing how we see fit, okay? We know what we're doing." Or did they? Ever since she and Jase had met up at Lana's wedding, their lives had become increasingly muddled and troublesome, and nothing they did seemed to fix things.

Now it was Will's turn to mumble something.

"Pardon me?" Millicent said. "You'll have to speak up."

"I just said, you haven't handled things real great so far. Go ahead, yell at me."

Why? Millicent thought. He'd only said aloud what she'd been thinking. "Sometimes," she said, looking at her son in the rearview mirror, "it's best to keep your thoughts to yourself—even when you know you're right."

Instead of pulling the van all the way into the garage, Millicent stopped in the driveway. She needed to see Mary Jane without delay. She'd never had such a problem with separation anxiety with any of her other kids.

Becky lay on the couch reading a book with the baby snoozing tucked up against her. Lily was on the floor, beating on a toy xylophone.

Millicent dropped her purse onto the floor with a thud, and Becky looked up with a start. "So, I suppose you don't know anything about this match-making plot?" Millicent said without preamble.

"Um . . . you're back early," Becky said innocently, raising herself up gingerly so as not to disturb Mary Jane. "Did you have fun?"

Will rolled his eyes and made a beeline for his room. Nancy shrugged as if to say, "I did my best," then slunk away too.

"I take it that means the plan backfired."

"Becky, you mean to tell me you were a part of this insane scheme? I was hoping to discover that it was mere coincidence you stopped by when you did."

"What can I say? I thought it was a good idea. You and Jase are meant for each other."

"Apparently not." Millicent crossed to the sofa and picked Mary Jane up, drawing comfort from her soft warmth and the smell of baby shampoo in her blond peach fuzz. "Is that meat loaf I smell?"

"Yeah, it's about ready to come out of the oven."

"Good. I'm starving. For some reason, that all-you-can-eat pizza buffet didn't fill me up."

As Jase pulled his car into the garage he realized he was weary down to the bone. No reason for it except that his brief meeting with Millicent had put him through a ringer.

"Dad, I'm sorry," Valerie said for about the twentieth time. "I thought you all would be happy that Nancy and I like each other now. She's really pretty cool."

"I'm thrilled beyond belief that you have a new friend. Let's leave it at that, okay?" Until now Jase had managed to rein in his temper. But he was right on the edge, and if Valerie didn't stop pushing . . .

"Okay, Dad." She hopped out of the car, followed by Heather, who hadn't said a word during the entire drive home. Poor Heather, Jase caught himself thinking. She was the sensitive one, the one who burst into tears the moment anyone raised their voice. She was the worrier, the peacemaker. And she was probably much more upset than her volatile sister.

He would talk to her later. To both of them. When he was calmer. Right now he needed to soak in the hot tub.

Saundra was in the laundry room ironing while Ginger sat on the washing machine with her favorite rag doll, offering advice. Jase greeted them both, then stopped at the fridge to get a beer. Just before popping it open, he changed his mind. For the next day and a half he would take exceptional care of his body. No alcohol, no caffeine, plenty of sleep, three nutritious squares a day, and he would find the time to swim his usual laps. He wanted to be in tip-top physical condition for Mary Jane's surgery.

Sure, he thought derisively as he eased into the swirling, steaming water in his giant bathtub, his body was a temple. It was his mind that was totally trashed.

He'd thought he could do it. He'd thought he could physically separate himself from Millicent, and with his customary mental discipline he could banish all thoughts of her from his mind. It had worked with Libby. When their marriage had been in a downhill slide, he'd been able to turn off his worries like a water faucet when it came to his work. Even when she'd been ill, then dying, he'd possessed the ability to divorce himself from the emotional trauma.

He wasn't having the same success with Millicent. Since their "talk" last week, he'd been feeling worse day by day, not better. He wasn't sleeping well, his concentration was shot, his stomach churned. Yet he couldn't back out of the surgery now. Millicent had placed too much faith in him. She believed in him. Responding to her faith in him, he'd even gone out of his way to tell her Mary Jane would be fine, when he didn't know that at all.

He'd sworn he wasn't going to do that. But seeing the desolation on her face, in the way she stood with her shoulders hunched and her arms folded protectively across her chest, he'd felt compelled to say something to give her hope.

And then she'd gone and turned the tables on him by reassuring him. She was the one who could lose her child, yet she'd been thinking of him, of his feelings. She was an incredible woman. And he loved her with every bone in his body.

He did. He loved her madly. And saying he didn't, pretending it was over between them, didn't change that simple fact.

He had to do something. Decisively, he turned off the jets and stood, letting the water drip from his body. He needed to take some kind of action, to reconcile the recent events in his life so they would mesh better rather than clashing together like discordant cymbals.

Clothes. He started to throw on any old thing, then thought better of it and chose with more care. He, at least, would remember the coming minutes and hours for the rest of his life. He didn't want to look like a slob on this important occasion. He put on his newest jeans, which Saundra insisted on ironing with sharp creases despite his objections, and a never-worn, mauve polo shirt. He combed his hair. He even shaved and slapped on a little English Leather. What the hell.

The drive to Millicent's house hardly registered with him. He rehearsed in his mind what he would say to her. But nothing seemed right; every phrase he chose seemed trite, like dialogue from a B movie.

He gave up rehearsing, trusting that the right words would come to him when it was time.

He almost lost his nerve as he approached the cozy farmhouse with its rambling additions and old-fashioned screen porch. A light burned inside, beckoning. But how could he face her after he'd caused her so much pain? How could he convince her he'd made a terrible mistake, when he'd put so much thought into making her believe the exact opposite?

He'd take his chances. If he didn't tell her how he felt, he wouldn't be able to sleep. And he had to sleep, dammit. He wished he could sleep with her, but he supposed that was out of the question.

Well, no use delaying this any further, he thought as he threw his car in park and switched off the engine. This was his moment of truth, Judgment Day.

Nancy answered the door. She took one look at him, gasped, and covered her mouth in a classic gesture of shock. But her eyes danced merrily.

"Mom!" she called out. "You have a visitor!" Then to Jase, "Come in, Dr. Desmond. Don't mind the mess, it isn't always like this. We're usually a little neater."

Jase smiled as he stepped over an obstacle course of baby toys just to get into the living room.

"Who is it, Nancy?" Millicent called from someplace that sounded far away. Her voice sent a pleasurable shiver up and down his spine.

"She's making pots," Nancy explained to Jase without answering her mother. "You can go on back. Down that hall, second door on the left. Surprise her. She'll like it."

Jase knew his visit would be surprising, but he had no idea whether Millicent's reaction would be pleasant or not. But it was too late to second-guess his decision now. He followed Nancy's directions. The second door was cracked open, and he slowly widened the gap until he revealed the heart-stopping image of Millicent, sitting at her potter's wheel, her hands gracefully molding clay into a tall, fluted vase. She was so absorbed in her work that she didn't look up, didn't notice him, and he took the opportunity to study her.

She looked so lovely, it squeezed his heart, even with her hair escaping from the baseball cap she was wearing, and a smudge of clay on her cheek.

"Hi, Millie."

She looked up, obviously startled, then embarrassed. She said nothing, just stared at him, waiting for him to make the first move.

"Sorry I didn't warn you I was coming," he began, "but I was afraid that if I called you, you would have told me not to come." He paused. "Would you have?"

"I don't know," she said cautiously. "It depends on what you want. Is it something about Mary Jane's surgery?"

"Indirectly." He had a feeling that if he hadn't fudged that answer, she'd have thrown him right out. He could already see that his visit was causing her discomfort. He hoped that by the time he left, she would feel differently. "Could we talk somewhere? Maybe go for a walk outside? It's a beautiful night."

"All right," she said warily, wiping her hands on a cloth. "Sorry I'm so—"

"It's okay. You look beautiful to me."

She blushed, but she didn't smile. In fact, she

wore a decided frown as she covered her work-in-progress with plastic.

She turned off the lights and led him back down the hall to the living room. "We can sit out on the porch if you like. Or walk down to the barn. I'll show you what the kids and I have done to prepare for our new horse."

"You're getting a horse?" he asked, surprised. He'd have thought something that frivolous would have been put on hold until the family's current crisis was over.

"She's the coolest thing," said Nancy, who'd obviously overheard his question as they entered the living room. "She's a brown and white paint, and her name's Sassy. She's coming next week. She's real gentle, and she even let Lily ride her."

"That's terrific," Jase said. "Sounds like you kids will have a lot of fun." And Millicent a lot of work, but he supposed she knew what she was doing.

"We're going for a walk," Millicent told Nancy. "Hold down the fort for a few minutes, okay?"

"Sure, Mom," Nancy answered breezily, a speculative gleam in her eye. "Stay out as long as you want. Everything's under control."

It really was a spectacular evening—cool for June, just the slightest breeze. The air smelled fresher out in the country, like freshly turned earth and green, growing things. And Millicent. He fancied he could smell her baby-powder scent, though maybe that was his imagination working overtime.

He said nothing for a while, letting the two of them simply adjust to each other's presence. He could sense Millicent's tension, her expectancy.

They walked around the back of the house and across the pasture, the same one the ambulance had driven through the night Mary Jane was born. The grass was high now, wet with dew, which quickly dampened the legs of his jeans. Millicent, in shorts and tennis shoes, seemed impervious to it.

A country girl. He had so much to learn about her.

"This is it," she said, pulling open the big double doors of the old-fashioned barn and ushering him inside. She fumbled along one wall, finally connecting with a light switch. A yellow lightbulb came on overhead. "I hired a carpenter to revamp a couple of stalls. Then we put in a feed trough, and some packed sand for the flooring. Then this is the tack room, where we'll keep saddles and blankets and such. The oats go in here, in this rodent-proof container. There's even a loft for hay, and an old hand-cranked conveyor belt."

"Sounds like you've put some thought into this," Jase remarked.

"We threw ourselves into the project," Millicent confessed. "It kept us busy, kept our minds off our troubles. Sassy's a beautiful horse. The kids talked me out of a pony because they would outgrow it too soon, and they're right." Her deluge of words sputtered to a stop. She looked around self-consciously, twisting her fingers together, then shoving her hands into the pockets of her shorts. "So, why are you here?"

"Because I couldn't stay away."

She closed her eyes, as if warding off his words.

"I thought I knew what I was doing. Obviously I don't. I thought I would feel calmer, less involved, if we broke things off. I don't. I've been going slowly crazy trying to convince myself I can get along without you. The truth is, I can't do it."

She was frighteningly silent. He wished she would give him a clue, any small sign, that she understood, that she agreed. Instead she walked over to a weather-beaten bench and sat down, pulled off her baseball cap, and ran her fingers through her fine, soft hair.

"I made a mistake," he said, plunging ahead. "I love you, Millicent. I want you to be my wife."

TEN

Millicent grew very still, almost afraid to breathe for fear Jase's words would somehow disintegrate. He loved her? He loved her! The realization caused a blossom of pure joy to bloom within her chest. Then the second part of his declaration registered. He wanted a wife. Marriage. Jase and her and seven kids under one roof. Ronnie's memory thrown out the window like last week's *TV Guide*.

All of these thoughts and feelings flashed through her mind in milliseconds, and she experienced a strong urge to run, to simply flee into the darkness to avoid having to acknowledge the statements hanging in the air between them.

Jase sat down beside her, though he didn't touch her. "Well?" he asked, his voice husky, seductive. "I've just bared my soul, thrown myself on your mercy, and you don't have anything to say?"

She jumped up and started pacing. She couldn't

think when he was so near. "I don't know what to say. Give me a minute to sort it out."

He grew more serious. "If you feel it's too soon, we can wait a while. You've had a lot to adjust to in a very short time—"

"No kidding," she retorted. Then she came to an abrupt halt and faced him, her hands on her hips. For the first time she looked straight at him. The open hopefulness in his eyes nearly undid her. At the same time, it made her angry—angry that he was forcing her to make this choice.

"Jase, what about all that stuff you said the other day, about needing to be detached and impersonal to be the best surgeon you can be? What about ethics?"

He sighed. "I'm not detached, and I'm not going to be. Nothing on God's green earth will change the way I feel about you and your kids."

Oh, the temptation. Millicent wanted to believe him. Such masterful rationalization. But she couldn't escape one thought: If she and Jase married, Mary Jane would be his daughter—stepdaughter, but that wouldn't make any difference to him. He would love her as one of his own. How could he possibly operate on her knowing that? How could he possibly cut into that child with a scalpel, knowing that, if he lost her, he would have to live with the reminder of it the rest of his life? She would become not just a patient he'd lost—which was horrible enough—but a member of his own family.

"I need to tell you something, Millicent," he said when she didn't respond. "It's about Libby."

Grateful for the reprieve, Millicent leaned against one of the stall doors, a safe distance from him, and nodded, indicating she was listening.

"When Libby died, it was tough on me for more reasons than just that she was my wife, the mother of my children. Any husband would hate watching his wife die slowly, by agonizing degrees. But I was a doctor, dammit. I should have been able to save her, somehow. I promised her I would save her. And I failed."

His pain was a palpable thing, assaulting her. She closed her mind against it. "I'm sure you did everything possible." The sentiment sounded trite. He'd probably heard it a thousand times.

"I did. But I'm not sure Libby believed that. You see, our marriage had been anything but ideal those last few years. She thought . . ." He seemed to be struggling for the words.

Millicent held her breath.

"She thought that if I'd loved her more, I could have saved her somehow, worked a miracle. Her last words to me were bitter, hurtful."

"Whatever she said, I'm sure she didn't mean it," Millicent said. "She was no doubt frightened, hurting, lashing out at any easy target who would shoulder the blame." Even as she mouthed the feeble attempt at comfort, her mind was racing. Why was he telling her this now?

An awful thought occurred to her. Was Mary

Jane his ticket to salvation? A chance to make up for his inability to save Libby's life?

Or another opportunity to punish himself?

"I shouldered the blame, all right. I accepted any and all guilt she wanted to heap on me. It took me a long time to realize, to really believe, that none of it was my fault. I guess what I'm trying to say . . . hell, I don't know. All I know is that I've been miserable since we broke things off. All that stuff I spouted off about ethics and detachment—I think it was to mask my fear, the fear that I would disappoint someone who was counting on me. Someone who loved me, but who would stop loving me if I messed up."

"But I would never—" She stopped herself. Easy, Millie. Watch what you say. One false step and she would be in the worst kind of hot water— the kind she'd boiled herself.

"I wouldn't blame you if you wanted to change your mind about me doing the operation," Jase said. "You can, you know. Dr. Boynton—"

"Jase, just answer one question. Do you believe you can do the surgery properly?"

"Yes," he answered without hesitation. "I've studied Mary Jane's tests, her MRIs, her CT scans, until they're burned into my brain. I know everything that's ever been learned about spinal tumors in general, and her case specifically. And my hand is steady as a rock."

"Then do it. Be the best damn doctor you can

be, and save your patient's life if you possibly can. I know you'll do that."

"I will. Is that all you have to say?"

She turned to face the stall, unable to look at him. "Yes."

"You're saying you don't love me?"

She hesitated. It was much easier to lie, but somehow she couldn't bring herself to do it, not when Jase had been so painfully honest with her, laying it all on the line, risking everything. "I will teach myself not to love you. It's the way it has to be, Jase." Too much of what he'd said the other day made sense. The fewer emotions riding on the surgery's outcome, the better. She absolutely would not have him thinking about *her* hopes, *her* disappointments, or how bad he would feel having to face her every day for decades to come.

She was tempted to put him on hold, to let herself think about it. Even if she didn't agree to marriage, committing her love was a huge decision. But instinctively she knew it was now or never. If she waited until after the surgery, her motives for changing her mind would always be suspect. If Mary Jane recovered, would he think she was giving her love out of gratitude or obligation? And if the worst happened . . . no. She couldn't sentence him to a lifetime of living with that. Libby had punished him enough for any one man.

Theodora had been wrong—it was that simple. Maybe Jase was the man who could make Millicent happy. But the fortuneteller apparently didn't foresee the circumstances under which they would meet. This wasn't their time.

"Then I guess that's all there is to say." Jase stood, his back stiff, his face immobile. "I'll see myself to my car. Please try to get some rest before Thursday."

"Yes, I will."

She stayed in the barn; he left. When she was sure he was far enough away, she dissolved into tears, her sobs echoing in the empty space.

Jase knew he'd blown it. He'd oversold her on his ethical dilemma in the first place. Now the damage couldn't be undone. He had no one to blame but himself.

There was only one thing left to do. He would try to save Mary Jane's life with every muscle in his body, every neuron in his brain. It was the one thing he had left to give Millicent. If the baby lived, if she recovered, knowing he'd helped would go a long way toward soothing the pain of her mother's absence from his life. If Mary Jane could lead a normal life, at least Millicent would remember him fondly.

The awesome responsibility should have frightened him. Instead he felt a surge of strength flowing through him. He would follow her advice. He would do his level best to cure his patient. And whatever happened, he would at least know that he'd done everything in his power to save her.

Jase went home and talked to Heather and Valerie, reassuring the girls that he wasn't angry anymore, that he understood that they'd been trying to do a good thing. He read Ginger a bedtime story and helped her say her prayers. At the same time, he made his own prayer, thanking God that his own children were healthy.

Finally he went to bed. He lay there for a few minutes, feeling the pain, the hollow ache where his heart should have been. And then he slept, long and hard, for the first time in he didn't know how long.

The next night Millicent didn't sleep much. She'd taken Mary Jane to the hospital that afternoon so that she could be tested, observed, and prepped for the grueling surgery the following morning.

She'd put the other kids to bed early because tomorrow would be a long day. But she couldn't find sleep herself. In the end she got up, went into the nursery, and pulled the baby quilt out of the crib.

She brought it to her face. It smelled like Mary Jane. She sank into her bentwood rocker and cradled the blanket and stared at the empty bed. Would she come home? Would she ever again sleep in her crib, with her Winnie-the-Pooh mobile spinning overhead and the windup chimes that soothed her to sleep?

Was she sleeping now, or did the strange surroundings and people upset her too much?

She thought of Jase too. Turning him away had been painful. But she was grateful for the time she'd had with him, brief though it was. He'd helped her through those last stages of grief over Ronnie. She didn't feel guilty anymore for making love with him. In fact, she almost believed that Ronnie, wherever he was, knew and approved. He'd been a generous, kindhearted, and fair man in life.

Eventually she fell asleep in the rocker, but it was a restless sleep. Strange dreams plagued her. The weirdest featured Theodora. "One will bury her man in a hickory grove," the fortuneteller said. "But all will find marriage a treasure trove, with a little help from above."

Millicent awoke with a start, almost expecting to see the woman in red sequins standing before her in real life, the dream had been so vivid. The poem. She'd forgotten the exact words. In fact, so had Callie and Lana. The three of them had tried to recall it once, and couldn't, although they remembered the gist of the predictions.

If ever she needed help from above, this was the time, she thought. "Theodora," she whispered. "If you're out there, I appreciate what you've done. And if you're . . . you know, an angel or something, do you think you could put in a good word for my baby?"

Silence met her request. She felt utterly foolish, but she'd had to try, just in case. Whether Theodora was an angel, a witch, or a collective figment of their imaginations, her appearance eleven years earlier had to have meant something. Maybe she was simply fate's way of nudging three hapless, confused girls in the right direction.

Millicent dozed off, then woke again around five, when the first glow of predawn was peeking through the window. Knowing she would sleep no more, she got up, replaced the quilt in the crib, and retreated to her bathroom for a shower. When she was dressed, she went to the kitchen and made a huge breakfast that she figured probably no one would eat, but cooking was good therapy.

The kids got up at six without a whimper, full of nervous tension. Millicent's mother had urged her to leave them at home, that they didn't need to be exposed to the hair-pulling tedium of a hospital waiting room. Millicent had read between the lines, too, understanding what her mother hadn't said. If Mary Jane died, her siblings should hear the news in the comfort of their own home, from their mother, not in some impersonal waiting room from a detached medical person.

Perhaps it was selfish, but Millicent wanted all of her children around her. They'd become quite a team over the past few months. She drew strength from them, and they from her. Besides, they would have been furious if she'd excluded them from this final trial.

Breakfast went largely untouched, as predicted. Millicent didn't press. She chugged down some orange juice, then instructed the children to gather up a few of their favorite books and toys. Within a few minutes everyone was in the van, and they were headed toward Methodist Medical Center.

"She spent a quiet, restful night," Mary Jane's nurse told the family. With a start, Millicent realized it was Robin Milhaus, Jase's escort from Lana's wedding, the one who'd invited them all to the lake. That seemed so long ago, yet it had only been a few weeks. "You can visit with Mary Jane for a few minutes before she goes to the O.R."

"Thank you," Millicent said, meaning it.

She and the kids crowded into what basically amounted to a hallway, where Mary Jane lay on a gurney. She had an I.V. tube in her foot, but it didn't seem to bother her. She smiled up at her mommy with obvious delight.

"You're such a good baby," Nancy cooed.

"Good baby," Lily echoed.

Will just stroked Mary Jane's arm, his face solemn.

All too soon she was taken away, and Millicent and the rest of the kids were left to the torturous oblivion of waiting. Millicent didn't watch the TV blaring in one corner of the room. She didn't read the book she'd brought with her, or the magazines that littered the coffee table. Her parents and Becky arrived, and they spent a good twenty minutes trying to be cheerful, but they gave up when Millicent replied to their questions with monosyllables, or not at all.

Finally they left her alone, and she stared down at her lap and let images of two people she loved very much wash through her mind. Mary Jane and Jase. Their fates were intertwined now. Millicent knew then that she couldn't survive losing them both. Oh, she might survive physically, but she would be an empty shell. A woman could handle only so much loss.

Jase surveyed the small, inert bundle before him on the table, made even smaller by all the sterile drapes shrouding it. He'd been preparing for this moment for a long time, and he felt amazingly ready. He had assembled the best surgical team that could be had. He had the latest technology at his fingertips. He was well rested and alert.

As for emotional detachment . . . he'd failed at that. He knew that if Mary Jane's recovery was anything less than perfect, he would live with that for eternity. But rather than hindering, his added stake in the procedure had given him an edge. It was almost as if something supernatural was surging through his body, enhancing his abilities.

"Is everyone ready? Everyone know his or her job?"

All the members of the team gave a reassuring "Yes."

"Then let's begin."

Millicent saw Dr. Boynton first, and her heart actually stopped beating. It was over. Four hours, twenty-three minutes. The doctor's face was neutral, exhaustion plain around his eyes.

She hopped out of her chair, searching in vain for some sign of Jase. But Dr. Boynton was alone.

"She came through the surgery," he said. His tone didn't invite optimism, but this was one hurdle crossed. Millicent said a quick prayer of thanks.

"Dr. Desmond was able to remove the tumor?" she asked, again holding her breath.

"Yes. He performed brilliantly, and the tumor has been sent to pathology. We'll know in a couple of days whether it's . . ." He looked cautiously at the children, who were hanging on his every word, then back at Millicent.

"It's okay," Millicent said. "I've told them everything I know."

"We'll know then whether it's cancer or not."

"What do you think?" she asked. She'd gotten pretty good at putting doctors on the spot, forcing them to be honest.

"Well . . . the growth did not bear what I think of as signs of malignancy, but of course we won't know for sure until—"

"Yes, I understand." Another hurdle crossed. Dr. Boynton would not have given her an optimistic opinion unless he was pretty confident the tumor was benign. "And what is her condition now?"

"She'll be in the I.C.U. for at least a couple of days. All we can do is watch and wait at this point."

"Can I see her?"

"I'll take you to the I.C.U. As soon as she's

stabilized they'll let you in. Only one family member at a time, though, and I'm afraid the children are, er, *verboten*."

"I'll go alone, then." All she wanted was a glimpse. She knew Mary Jane would probably not be conscious yet. But if Millicent could see her eyelashes flutter, or hear a little sigh, she would feel better.

On the way to the I.C.U. she got up the nerve to ask Dr. Boynton, "Where's Jase?"

"He stayed with his patient. Very dedicated man. I'm glad you took my advice. It's gratifying to realize such a gifted surgeon got his start with me."

Millicent's pain, so familiar now, settled around her heart. She struggled to keep her voice unemotional. "He speaks highly of you too."

They arrived in the I.C.U. at almost the same time as Mary Jane's gurney. It rushed past them, hardly giving Millicent a chance even to see the baby. Jase was right behind it. If he saw Millicent, he didn't acknowledge her. His focus was on the baby.

Dr. Boynton left her in yet another waiting area, giving Millicent more time than she needed to obsess. By turning down Jase's proposal, turning away his love, had she alienated him forever?

That was the general idea, she thought, frowning. She'd made her choices, choices that had seemed the best of her difficult options. How selfish of her to question those decisions. Yet she did.

"Mrs. Jones?" A nurse appeared before her. "You can come this way."

Mary Jane's "room" was an open bay across from the nurse's station. Robin and another nurse were fussing over the frightening array of wires and tubes attached to the tiny bundle that was her daughter. And there was Jase, hovering with a proprietary air. Dedicated, yes, as Dr. Boynton had said. But something else.

He loved Mary Jane, and he was agonizing over her condition as sharply as a father would have. As Ronnie would have.

The realization hit her in the stomach like a brickbat. By turning Jase away, she'd accomplished nothing. Had she thought Jase was a machine, that he could become detached from a child he cared for simply because Millicent had dictated that he would?

What had she done to him? By practically forcing him to do the surgery, she'd dumped a responsibility on him that no man should have to bear. He should rightfully resent her for eternity.

She approached the bed cautiously, desperate for a glimpse of her child, but she didn't want to in any way hinder the medical team's efficiency.

Jase looked up. She did not see resentment in his eyes. She saw love, and pain, and exhaustion.

"Millicent."

"How is she?"

He sighed. "Weak. Her vital signs are erratic. The next few hours will be important."

"Dr. Boynton said the surgery itself went well—that you did a fantastic job."

"He's too humble. It was a team effort. And yes, I feel good about the job we did." He said this with not a hint of conceit, just quiet pride.

"I wanted to thank you."

He looked away. "No thanks necessary," he said, bitterness creeping into his voice. "It's my job."

"It's more than—"

A thin wailing cut her off. Mary Jane was stirring, fretting. Millicent went to the bed, a sob escaping from her own throat as she did. She forgot her intention to stay out of the way. Robin made some adjustments, cooing reassuringly.

"There, there, sweetheart. You'll be fine. Your mama's here. Millicent, why don't you come around here where Mary Jane can see your face. There's nothing more comforting to an infant."

Millicent did as she was asked, speaking in soft tones, trying to smile, to reassure, although the sight of all those wires and tubes and needles and restraints weren't reassuring in the least. Maybe it was her imagination, but the baby's tiny, pale face seemed to focus on her. Millicent could almost feel Mary Jane's pain. But the baby did quiet down as she gazed at her mother, looking more confused than anything.

"How long can I stay?" she asked, looking to Jase, then Robin.

"Ten minutes every hour," was the nurse's no-nonsense answer.

That meant her first ten minutes were almost up. The nurses both retreated, leaving Millicent and Jase as alone as they could be in a frenetic I.C.U. "Will you stay with me until they kick me out?" she asked Jase. "Then I'd like to talk to you, someplace private, if you have time."

"Of course I have time. I blocked the whole day just for Mary Jane."

"Do you normally do that?" she asked.

He didn't answer, but his silence spoke for him. Mary Jane was not just any patient to him.

They sat in silence, on opposite sides of the bed, surrounded by the whir and beep of the medical equipment. Jase checked the various screens and gauges, his forehead creased with worry lines. Millicent kept her gaze on Mary Jane, who slept fitfully. She tried to ignore the erratic noises coming from the machines. She didn't know what they meant, and her imagination would drive her crazy if she let it.

Eventually Robin returned, clearing her throat. She'd already let Millicent stay a good twenty minutes. With a sigh Millicent said good-bye to Mary Jane, made a few extravagant promises, then forced herself to walk out.

Jase murmured a few last-minute instructions to the nurses, then he was right behind Millicent. They walked, not talking, no destination in mind. They ended up outside, where a sultry summer day was in full swing. A park bench under an old tree beckoned, and they sat down.

"I made a terrible mistake," Millicent said abruptly. "I was trying to play God. I thought I knew what was best—"

"*You're* playing God?" Jase exploded. "I'm the one who just performed surgery on a little girl I couldn't love more if she were my own daughter." He looked at Millicent, a little sheepishly. "There, I've admitted it."

"And I'm the one who made you do it," she said quietly. "I didn't understand what I was asking. I thought it would be easier on you if you knew the Jones family wasn't to be a part of your future. But it didn't work that way, did it?"

"No." The single word tore at her heart.

"Thank you again for shouldering an awesome responsibility. I'm deeply sorry I put you through such an ordeal. I guess I underestimated how much you care for Mary Jane. But I'm not sorry you did the surgery. Because I know, with absolute certainty, that you wouldn't have cut on my baby if you weren't a hundred percent sure of your ability to do what needed to be done."

He nodded in acknowledgment.

"Can we, um, renegotiate?"

Jase looked at her blankly. "Renegotiate what?"

"That marriage proposal. I'm still a little stunned at the idea of marriage. It's a huge step, and I'm not sure I'm ready. But I am sure that the reasons I didn't want to marry you were stupid and faulty. Want to give it another whirl? I'll give you a more rational answer this time."

She held her breath. Although she'd tried to sound saucy and confident, breezy, she was a mass of insecurity. She wouldn't blame him if he was so disgusted with her wishy-washy decisions that he walked away without a word.

"I don't know, Millie. I'm afraid we've reached a point where we can't undo—"

"But we can talk about it?" she asked hopefully, her heart beating as fast as a hummingbird's.

He hesitated. "Millie, maybe now isn't such a great time to be making life-altering decisions. We've both been through a lot."

He's changed his mind, she immediately thought. She'd blown it. "I've never been more sure of anything," she tried again, because she wasn't giving up without a fight. She was going to state her case firmly, clearly. "I love you, Jase. I know I can get through anything if I'm with you."

Funny, but she'd imagined his face lighting up with joy when she declared her love. Instead he looked as if he'd just received devastating news.

"What if Mary Jane had died during surgery?" Jase asked, his voice barely a whisper. "Would we be having this conversation? I can't help but think your feelings are tied up somehow with this heroic image you have of me—Jase Desmond, life-saving surgeon."

"Oh, Jase." He had it all wrong. "I admire your skill as a doctor. Who wouldn't? But that's not why

I love you. I love you because of the way you took in my whole family at a time when we needed you most. I love you because you wouldn't give up on me, stubborn ninny that I am. I love you because you never, for one moment, resented Ronnie's memory. And I love you because, well, because I saw the way you looked at my daughter in the I.C.U. I saw how much you care. And I knew, at that moment, that I would never find a more loving husband and father."

He looked at her as if he wanted to believe her. But something was obviously still troubling him. "Mary Jane still could die, you know."

"Yes, I know." She'd come to terms with that possibility.

"If she survives, she could be impaired. We won't have any idea of her degree of recovery for several days, until the swelling goes down."

"I know that too. My feelings for you aren't tied to her survival." She paused, weighing her words carefully. "I'm not like Libby. I would never blame you for something you ultimately can't control. And, frankly, though I know she is the mother of your children, and I never even met the woman, I dislike her intensely for blaming you for her death. How could she be so cruel?"

Suddenly embarrassed by the rush of hot accusations, Millicent cleared her throat. "I'm sorry. Maybe there's a little jealousy at work here too. Guess I'm not as gracious about Libby as you are about Ronnie."

Jase surprised her by laughing.

"Did I say something funny?"

"No. It's just that, if you only knew how much I've held back. You aren't the only one who's been jealous and resentful. It's pretty hard to compete with a sainted memory. I mean, didn't the man do *anything* bad?"

"Well . . ." Millicent had to think a few moments. "He always left the toilet seat up."

They looked at each other, and all at once they were laughing and hugging. Millicent laughed and cried at the same time until she had no strength left. Then Jase kissed her, with so much aching tenderness that she was moved to tears again. Her daughter was lying in intensive care, her life hanging by a thread, yet oddly Millicent felt better than she had in a long time. Love, whether she was giving or receiving, had that effect on her. She was getting a good dose of the healing effects right now.

"Does this mean negotiations are officially reopened?" she asked breathlessly.

"What do you think?" He stared into her eyes until she thought she would drown in the love pouring out of him. Then he frowned and said, "Oh my God."

"What?"

"We'll have seven children. Seven. Where will we put them all?"

Millicent smiled with relief. She'd thought something really was wrong. "Room additions," she said. "It's always worked for me."

EPILOGUE

"Wow, Millicent, you look like a princess," Callie exclaimed. She sat in a corner of the bride's room, nursing her newborn one last time before the wedding ceremony.

"An angel," Lana amended. "So serene."

"Then I must be a very good actress." Millicent eyed herself critically in the full-length mirror. She'd chosen a gown in a deep champagne color, and Becky had insisted on a matching hat. Now she was having doubts about the hat.

"You're nervous?" Becky asked.

"How could I not be? The hat's not me," she declared.

"Don't you dare take it off," Lana said. "You can't walk down the aisle bareheaded."

"Lana, that sounds like something your mother would have said," Callie admonished. "Millicent can do anything she wants. It's her wedding."

"Oh, I suppose I'll keep the hat on. I went all the way to Dallas to buy it and paid eighty-six dollars for the darned thing."

The door to the bride's room opened a crack, and Millicent's mother peeked in. "Okay if I bring in a few visitors?"

Millicent checked to see that Callie was decently clad, then smiled broadly. "The more the merrier." She opened her arms wide as Lily, resplendent in a lilac flower-girl's dress, burst in. Ginger, in identical garb, was close behind. Millicent's mother herded in the rest of the kids—all but Mary Jane. Before she knew it, Millicent was enveloped in hugs and kisses from the two flower girls as well as Heather and Nancy.

Will hung back. He was still getting used to the idea of being the only boy in such a large crowd of female children, but he got along well with the Desmond girls, especially quiet, sensitive Heather.

"You look awesome, Mom," Nancy said.

"Awesome," Valerie echoed. The two girls had become fast friends over the last few months, sometimes sounding like twins, they were so much alike. They'd even agreed to share a room.

"It's almost time," Millicent's mother said. Because Millicent had opted for a simple courthouse ceremony with Ronnie, her mother hadn't gotten a chance to do the big-wedding thing. Now she was making up for it in spades. She was running the show with a military precision Patton would have envied. "Becky, you're in charge of the flower girls.

Remember, start them down the aisle when the organist begins the processional. You girls will follow every thirty seconds, the way we rehearsed last night. Got it?"

"We've got it, Mrs. Whitney," Lana said with a sharp salute.

Millicent hid a smile. This was the fifth wedding in all for her and her two high school friends. They were getting pretty good at it.

"Callie, that darling husband of yours is waiting outside to take the baby. You older kids come with me. We'll have one of those handsome ushers take us to our seats, and we'll be ready."

The church was packed. As the bridesmaids assembled in the vestibule, Millicent caught a glimpse of Jase standing near the altar, waiting for her. He looked achingly handsome in his formal wear.

"So many people," Callie whispered.

"I don't even recognize half of them," Millicent whispered back. "Jase's family flew in from all over the country. I'll never learn all their names."

"Who's the floozy in the red dress?" Lana asked. "I assume she's not part of *your* fam—" She stopped suddenly.

"Which floozy? What's wrong?" Millicent asked.

"That woman! She looks like . . . no, that's silly."

Callie slipped her glasses out of her sleeve and put them on. "Where, what woman?"

"Over there!" Lana gestured dramatically.

"Doesn't she look familiar? Oh, darn, now she's turned away."

Millicent grew very still. She'd gotten a good look at the woman's face. And she did, indeed, look familiar.

The start of the processional music prevented any open conjecture. "Colonel Becky" dispatched the excited flower girls as ordered, and Millicent pushed thoughts of the woman in red out of her mind. She was marrying Jase Desmond. Her heart was so full, she thought it would burst.

Ginger and Lily scattered rose petals down the aisle, though Ginger paused to eat some of hers. A helpful guest herded the two little girls to the front. Then the three bridesmaids—Becky, Callie, and Lana, began their walks.

When Millicent started down the aisle, the congregation stood. Everyone beamed. Millicent had thought some people might express disapproval at a marriage so soon . . . but it wasn't that soon anymore, she supposed. And no one had seemed anything less than ecstatic over Millicent and Jase's engagement.

Millicent longed to glance to her left where the woman in red was sitting, but she didn't dare. If it really was Theodora, she might just faint.

She focused on Jase's face. He looked proud enough to burst his cummerbund. As she paused and took his arm Heather and Will, as rehearsed, straightened the train of her dress.

"Dearly beloved," the minister began. The ceremony went by in a whirl of nervously stammered vows, clumsily exchanged rings. Then, abruptly, it was over and they were married. The minister introduced them as a couple to the congregation, followed by thunderous applause.

On the walk up the aisle, Millicent searched the crowd for the woman in red. There she was! And there was no mistaking the gypsy woman's large, dark eyes, full lips, and curly black hair. She winked broadly and mouthed something to Millicent: *I told you so.* Then Jase whisked Millicent out of the church into the vestibule, and she lost sight of Theodora.

During the flurry of congratulatory hugs and kisses, Millicent craned her neck and looked all around.

"Sweetheart, is everything okay?" Jase asked, sounding concerned.

"Oh, yes! Oh, everything's fabulous. It's just that I thought I saw an old friend in the church, and now I don't see her."

"You *did* see an old friend," Callie said meaningfully. "And so did I. Now it appears she's vanished . . . again."

After all these years, for Theodora to reappear—what did it mean? Did she have more predictions for them? Another poem, perhaps? Or did she simply come to gloat?

"Yoo-hoo, Millie," Betty Desmond called, working her way through the crowd. "I have someone here who wants to give you a big kiss."

Mary Jane! Ever since Jase's mother had arrived in Destiny a week before, she'd taken charge of the baby, would hardly let anyone else touch her. She was tickled pink to suddenly have four new grand-children, but Mary Jane had obviously found a special place in Betty's heart.

When the baby had recovered from her surgery, it had become apparent that movement on the left side of her body was impaired. But her prognosis was excellent. Dr. Daas had said that with physical therapy and lots of hard work and patience, Mary Jane could recover completely.

Betty, a retired physical therapist, had taken charge of the baby's exercise routine, leaving Millicent with one less thing to worry about during this hectic week.

Millicent gathered Mary Jane into her arms and bussed her on the cheek. "Hello, my precious. You must have been a good girl during the wedding. I didn't hear any crying."

"She's an angel," Betty said, reclaiming the baby with a proprietary air.

The reception was in the church hall next door. First there were pictures to be taken, then an erratic receiving line to be endured. Millicent kept her eyes peeled for a flash of red. Just when she was beginning to think she'd imagined seeing the gypsy, The-odora was standing right in front of her, shaking her hand.

Millicent just stared, stunned. The woman hadn't aged a day in eleven years.

"Aren't you going to introduce me?" Jase asked, clearly charmed.

"Jase, this is Theodora, an old friend," Millicent said in a monotone. She was too shocked to do better.

"Very nice to meet you," Theodora said, flashing that maddeningly secret smile. "You must love children."

"Yes, I do," Jase said. "We both do."

"Good. A couple with eight children should have an affinity for them, don't you agree?"

"Oh, but we only have seven," Jase said.

Millicent simply gasped and placed a hand on her flat abdomen. Really, it was useless to argue with the gypsy.

Theodora winked. "I have just two words to say about that Mary Jane. Ballet lessons."

Before Millicent could recover, Theodora had moved down the line. "It must be nice, being married to the chief of police," she said to Lana, who gazed in openmouthed awe. "And you, the suspicious one," she said to Callie. "Have you cleared off a place on your mantel?"

"What for?" Callie asked, almost belligerently.

"For that Pulitzer Prize."

"But I'm not even—"

"Save it," Lana said, giggling, as Theodora moved out of hearing range. "You know she's right."

Callie pulled her glasses out of her sleeve and shoved them onto her face, which was a mask of determination. "She's not getting away this time. Ladies, are you with me?"

Millicent took a deep breath. Her mother would throw a fit, but she supposed this departure from wedding etiquette was inevitable. "Excuse us for a moment, would you, dear?" she said to Jase. "This won't take a minute." Before she could think too hard about what she was doing, she followed Lana and Callie through the crowded reception hall, in pursuit of a flash of red.

"This way," Callie called. She kicked off her pumps and broke into a run.

Murmuring, "Oh, my, this is so unseemly," Lana followed suit.

Millicent threw her train over her arm, hiked up her skirt, and joined the chase. She could see Theodora pushing her way through an emergency exit. Oddly, the alarm didn't go off. When the three friends reached the door, they followed without hesitation. This time an ear-piercing bell blasted through the once-peaceful reception hall.

They found themselves in a back parking lot. Theodora was nowhere to be seen. There were no cars exiting the parking lot. Nothing.

"She did it to us again," Callie fumed.

But Millicent laughed. "I don't think we're supposed to know too much about the mysterious Theodora."

"But who is she?" Callie persisted. "Some kind of witch?"

"I think she's an angel, sent to watch over us," Lana said.

"Or maybe she's just a regular person with a rare gift," Millicent offered. "Maybe she goes all over the world, helping people."

"You call that help?" Callie asked. "She said I would win a Pulitzer. Get real! I own a tiny, weekly paper in the middle of nowhere, where nothing happens."

"She told me Sloan would be chief of police someday," Lana said. "Well, either that or I'll divorce him and marry Chief Johnson, and I don't think that's very likely. Millicent, what did she say to you?"

Millicent sighed. She decided she would keep her news to herself for now. Jase should be the first to know that an eighth child was on the way, or soon would be. As for Mary Jane dancing ballet— no prediction could have made Millicent happier. Theodora had told her, in her own way, that her baby would make a full recovery.

"Let's go back inside before they send the National Guard out after us," Millicent suggested. "And then I think we should propose a toast. To the Theodora Club. We've been here for each other through thick and thin."

"Maybe that's all Theodora wanted to accomplish," Lana said thoughtfully as they headed back indoors. "Maybe she wanted us to learn that our friendship could get us through the rough spots. She's one of the reasons we've all remained such close friends, you know. We might have drifted apart, if not for sharing the secret of Theodora."

The reception line was a shambles, so Jase and Millicent gave up on it. The band was striking up a waltz, and couples drifted onto the dance floor.

"What's going on with you three?" Jase asked as he and Millicent danced. "You're acting very strangely. And who was that woman?"

"It's a long story," Millicent said with a smile. "I'll tell you about it later." Not that he would ever believe her, even if she showed him the old brown medicine bottle that bore his name. She'd always kept it.

"But—"

"Did you know that I love you, Dr. Desmond?"

Jase relented with a smile of his own. "Did you know I love *you*, Mrs. Desmond? More than words can say."

THE EDITORS' CORNER

Hey! Look out your window. What do you see? Summer's finally in full bloom! And what does that mean? It means you can grab your four new LOVE-SWEPTs and head outdoors to read them! So when you're at the beach, in the backyard, or sitting on the dock of the bay, take care not to get sunburned while you bask in the warm summer sun reading your LOVESWEPTs!

Remember Georgia DeWitt, the woman who was jilted at the altar in DADDY MATERIAL? Well, she's back in **GEORGIA ON HIS MIND**, LOVE-SWEPT #842, Marcia Evanick's second chapter of her White Lace & Promises trilogy. Carpenter Levi Horst knows he has no business fantasizing about a woman who's clearly out of his league, especially when she's his boss! Georgia knows she doesn't inspire men to move mountains—her last experience taught her that. But when she sets up her own antiques business and discovers a kindred spirit who shares her secret dreams, she's forced to reconsider. Now all she has to do is convince Levi that they really aren't from two different worlds after all. In a story sparkling with wit and tender sensuality, Marcia tells us what can happen when two unlikely lovers are astonished by their heart's desires and decide to risk it all to become a family.

In **TRUST ME ON THIS,** LOVESWEPT #843 from award-winning Jennifer Crusie, con-buster Alec Prentice and reporter Dennie Banks are thrown together by a whim of fate, but both have their own agendas in mind. After Alec is convinced that Dennie is not in cahoots with a notorious con man, he enlists her help in trapping his quarry. Dennie wants to interview a woman for a story that's guaranteed to earn her the promotion she so richly deserves—and she'll do anything to get it. After offending the woman she was supposed to interview, Dennie thinks it's time for plan B. Enter Alec, who has promised to help if she'll agree to his terms. Can these two passionate partners in crime get their man *and* each other? (Of course they can, it's a LOVESWEPT!) But *how* they do it is another thing. Find out how in Jennifer Crusie's hilarious and fast-paced gem of a love story!

Got a fire extinguisher? Looks like Jack Riley and Mary Jo Simpson are gonna need it when they meet in a classic case of **SPONTANEOUS COMBUSTION,** LOVESWEPT #844. Mary Jo seems to need a hero, but even after Jack has fought through fire to rescue her, he still insists he's no hero. She trembles at his touch, a touch that thrills her no end. But it scares her even more. She's lost every man she's ever loved to the line of duty and fears this man will be no different. When she becomes Jack's prime suspect in an arson investigation, Jack must decide if trusting his mystery lady could mean getting burned. LOVE-SWEPT favorite Janis Reams Hudson returns in a steamy saga of a man and a woman torn between their desire to do what's right and their desire for each other.

Nicole Sanders would rather get stuck in the mud than jump into the car with sexy stranger Alex Coleman in **TELL ME NO LIES**, LOVESWEPT #845 by rising star Jill Shalvis. Alone for most of her life, Nicole is bewildered to learn that she's been purposely denied the one thing she wants most—family. Now she has to wade through a sea of lies that will ultimately force her to make the hardest decision of her life. Alex has always been a sucker for a damsel in distress, and Nicole is no exception. As he fights the walls around her soul, the key to her identity may be all that stands between a future of love and a past full of sorrow and bitterness. In a powerful story of longing and belonging, Jill Shalvis entangles a woman desperate for love with a man who promises to be all the family she'll ever need.

Happy reading!

With warmest wishes,

Shauna Summers *Joy Abella*

Shauna Summers   Joy Abella
Editor   Administrative Editor

P.S. Look for these Bantam women's fiction titles coming in July. From *New York Times* bestselling author Nora Roberts comes a hardcover edition of **PUBLIC SECRETS,** a tale of a pop-music superstar's daughter who grows to womanhood amid secrets too painful to remember, too dangerous to forget. From Teresa Medeiros comes **TOUCH OF ENCHANTMENT,** the sequel to her national bestseller, BREATH OF MAGIC. The only thing Tabitha Lenox hates more than being a witch is being a rich witch. But when she finds a mysterious family heirloom, she is whisked back to an era of dragons, knights, magic—and love. Newcomer Annette Reynolds delivers **REMEMBER THE TIME,** a spellbinding romance full of emotion and passion, in the tradition of Fern Michaels. When Kate Armstrong's husband dies in a tragic accident, little does she know she will learn more about him in death than she ever did while he was alive. Can Kate overcome her grief to rediscover her true self and find the love and fulfillment she deserves?

For current information on Bantam's women's fiction, visit our new web site, ISN'T IT ROMANTIC, at the following address:

http://www.bdd.com/romance

Don't miss these extraordinary books by
your favorite Bantam authors

On sale in May

AFFAIR
by Amanda Quick

TWICE A HERO
by Susan Krinard

TEXAS WILDCAT
by Adrienne deWolfe

SWEET REVENGE
by Nora Roberts

AFFAIR

by
New York Times bestselling author

Amanda Quick

available in hardcover

*Charlotte Arkendale thinks she knows all there is
to know about men. But nothing in her
experience has prepared her for Baxter St. Ives. A
dedicated man of science, St. Ives finds himself
reluctantly embroiled in a murder investigation—
and at the mercy of a fierce and highly illogical
passion for Charlotte. Caught up in their web of
passion, the lovers are unaware that a killer stalks
them, plotting to separate them . . . or to see
them joined together forever—in death.*

"You leave me no option but to be blunt, Mr. St. Ives.
Unfortunately, the truth of the matter is that you are not
quite what I had in mind in the way of a man-of-affairs."
Charlotte Arkendale clasped her hands together on top
of the wide mahogany desk and regarded Baxter with a
critical eye. "I am sorry for the waste of your time."

The interview was not going well. Baxter adjusted the
gold-framed eyeglasses on the bridge of his nose and
silently vowed that he would not give in to the impulse
to grind his back teeth.

"Forgive me, Miss Arkendale, but I was under the im-
pression that you wished to employ a person who appeared completely innocuous and uninteresting."

"Quite true."

"I believe your exact description of the ideal candidate
for the position was, and I quote, *a person who is as bland
as a potato pudding*."

Charlotte blinked wide, disconcertingly intelligent, green eyes. "You do not comprehend me properly, sir."

"I rarely make mistakes, Miss Arkendale. I am nothing if not precise, methodical, and deliberate in my ways. Mistakes are made by those who are impulsive or inclined toward excessive passions. I assure you, I am not of that temperament."

"I could not agree with you more on the risks of a passionate nature," she said quickly. "Indeed, that is one of the problems—"

"Allow me to read to you precisely what you wrote in your letter to your recently retired man-of-affairs."

"There is no need. I am perfectly aware of what I wrote to Mr. Marcle."

Baxter ignored her. He reached into the inside pocket of his slightly rumpled coat and removed the letter he had stored there. He had read the damn thing so many times that he almost had it memorized, but he made a show of glancing down at the flamboyant handwriting.

"'As you know, Mr. Marcle, I require a man-of-affairs to take your place. He must be a person who presents an ordinary, unassuming appearance. I want a man who can go about his business unnoticed; a gentleman with whom I can meet frequently without attracting undue attention or comment.

"'In addition to the customary duties of a man-of-affairs, duties which you have fulfilled so very admirably during the past five years, sir, I must ask that the gentleman whom you recommend possess certain other skills.

"'I shall not trouble you with the details of the situation in which I find myself. Suffice it to say that due to recent events I am in need of a stout, keenly alert individual who can be depended upon to protect my person. In short, I wish to employ a bodyguard as well as a man-of-affairs.

"'Expense, as always, must be a consideration. Therefore, rather than undertake the cost of engaging two men to fill two posts, I have concluded that it will prove more economical to employ one man who can carry out the responsibilities of both positions—'"

"Yes, yes, I recall my own words quite clearly," Charlotte interrupted testily. "But that is not the point."

Baxter doggedly continued:

"'I therefore request that you send me a respectable gentleman who meets the above requirements and who presents an appearance that is as bland as a potato pudding.'"

"I fail to see why you must repeat aloud everything on the page, Mr. St. Ives."

Baxter pressed on:

"'He must be endowed with a high degree of intelligence as I shall require him to make the usual delicate inquiries for me. But in his capacity as a bodyguard, he must also be skilled in the use of a pistol in case events take a nasty turn. Above all, Mr. Marcle, as you well know, he must be discreet.'"

"Enough, Mr. St. Ives." Charlotte picked up a small volume bound in red leather and slapped it smartly against the desktop to get his attention.

Baxter glanced up from the letter. "I believe I meet most of your requirements, Miss Arkendale."

"I am certain that you do meet a few of them." She favored him with a frosty smile. "Mr. Marcle would never have recommended you to me if that were not the case. Unfortunately there is one very important qualification which you lack."

Baxter deliberately refolded the letter and slipped it back inside his coat. "You insisted upon a man who would draw little attention. A staid, unremarkable man-of-affairs."

"Yes, but—"

"Allow me to tell you that I am often described in those very terms. Bland as a potato pudding in every way."

Charlotte scowled. "Do not feed me that banbury tale. You most certainly are not a potato pudding. Just the opposite, in fact."

He stared at her. "I beg your pardon?"

She groaned. "You must know very well, sir, that your spectacles are a poor disguise."

"Disguise?" He wondered if he had got the wrong address and the wrong Charlotte Arkendale. Perhaps he had got the wrong town. "What in the name of the devil do you believe me to be concealing?"

"Surely you are not suffering from the illusion that those spectacles mask your true nature."

"My true nature?" Baxter lost his grip on his patience. "Bloody hell, just what am I, if not innocuous and unprepossessing?"

She spread her hands wide. "You have the look of a man of strong passions who has mastered his temperament with even stronger powers of self-mastery."

"I beg your pardon?"

Her eyes narrowed with grim determination. "Such a man cannot hope to go about unnoticed. You are bound to attract attention when you conduct business on my behalf. I cannot have that in my man-of-affairs. I require someone who can disappear into a crowd. Someone whose face no one recalls very clearly. Don't you understand, sir? You give the appearance of being rather, well, to be quite blunt, *dangerous*."

The nationally bestselling author of *Prince of Shadows* and *Star-Crossed* weaves a thrilling new tale of time travel, intrigue, and romantic adventure.

TWICE A HERO
by Susan Krinard

MacKenzie "Mac" Sinclair is cursed. So is the whole Sinclair family. Ever since her great-great-grandfather Peregrine returned from an expedition to the Mayan ruins with half of a mysterious pendant—and without his partner, Liam O'Shea—they've been haunted by misfortune. That's why Mac's beloved grandfather wants her to undertake a solo expedition . . . to return the pendant to the ruins of Tikal and find a way to atone for whatever part Peregrine played in Liam's disappearance. But when Mac braves the steamy, primitive jungle, something extraordinary happens: she blunders into the arms of an eerily familiar explorer. Now she's in for more adventure than she bargained for. Because she's found Liam O'Shea . . . alive, well, and seductively real. In the year 1884.

The woman was obviously an actress of considerable talent. Or she was quite mad.

"1884?" she repeated, her low voice hoarse. "Did you say—*1884?* But that's not possible."

Liam regarded her stunned expression with suspicious bemusement. Simple insanity did fit hand in glove with the rest of her: thin, wiry, distinctly peculiar with her cap of short hair and bold dark eyes, sharp-tongued, dressed top to toe in men's clothing of an odd cut, and carrying a newfangled electric lantern the likes of which he had never seen in all his travels. And alone here in the jungle, first claiming she'd been with a full party of explorers and then insisting that no man had brought her.

And then there were her odd manner of speech, her absurd assertions of hotels in the jungle and omnibuses from Flores, her reaction to Tikal—as if she'd expected to see something entirely different, though she claimed to know the ruins.

Yes, one could almost believe she was in a state of mental disturbance—if not for the photograph she had so carelessly allowed him to see. The one taken here in these very ruins four years ago.

"What did you expect, Miss MacKenzie?" he asked. "Maybe you've been in the jungle too long after all."

Her dark brows drew down, and her gaze grew unfocused. "Okay, Mac," she muttered. "Time to wake up. This isn't happening."

Was this act a way of protecting herself, avoiding his questions because she'd revealed too much? Liam couldn't forget the shock he'd felt when he'd seen her with the photograph. Until that moment she'd been only an unforeseen burden to dispose of in the nearest safe place, some eccentric suffragist amateur explorer who'd been lost or deliberately abandoned, left for him to save.

After what had happened yesterday, he'd never considered doing otherwise.

The sharp sting of recent memory made the bitterness rise in his throat: Perry's revelation, the knowledge that Liam's trust in his partner had been entirely misplaced, the fight, drinking to drown the rage and loss, waking up this morning to find the bearers, mules, and nearly all the supplies, gone. With Perry.

Abandoned. Betrayed by the one man he'd thought he could trust. The man who stood beside him in that damned photograph.

He'd thought the girl in far more desperate straits than himself. She was of the weaker sex, in spite of her ridiculous beliefs to the contrary. But now—now he felt a grinding suspicion in his gut, wild thoughts fully as mad as the woman's incoherent ramblings and disjointed explanations.

Liam scowled at Miss MacKenzie's inward stare. She wasn't the only one with wits gone begging. A woman? Even Perry wouldn't sink so far. And there hadn't been time. But after yesterday nothing seemed beyond possibility.

And their meeting had seemed more than merely coincidence.

He studied her, chin on fist, allowing himself full rein to his imagination. Perry would never assume that his erstwhile partner would be distracted by a woman like this. She was hardly beautiful. Her hair was ridiculously short, her brows too heavy, her stubborn jaw too strong, her figure too narrow. Though she'd proven she was, in fact, female enough when the rain had soaked through her shirt.

He found himself gazing at her chest. More there than he'd first noticed; come to think of it, she couldn't pass for a boy, not unless that loose shirt were completely dry. . . .

You've been without a woman too long, O'Shea. He snorted. *No.* At best Perry would expect him to be delayed further, getting the girl back to civilization. That would neatly fit in with his intentions.

Liam's fist slammed into the wet stone of the temple. Perry knew too damned much about him. He knew Liam wouldn't leave any woman alone in the jungle, no matter what his circumstances—without supplies or bearers or even a single scrawny mule. . . .

Because you trusted him. The rage bubbled up again, and with very little effort he could imagine his fist connecting with Perry's superior, aristocratic face.

By the saints, it wasn't over yet. When Liam got back to San Francisco—

"That's it."

He snapped out of his grim reverie. Miss MacKenzie—"Mac," the name she had called herself and which suited her so well—had apparently recovered her senses. Or ended her game. She was on her feet, looking out over the jungle with set jaw and a lunatic's obsession.

"I'm going back," she announced.

Liam rose casually. The top of her cropped head came almost to his chin; tall for a woman. He hadn't realized that before.

"Back where—'Mac'?" he drawled.

Her stare was no longer unfocused. She looked at him as if she'd like to pitch him over the side of the pyramid. "Only my friends call me Mac," she said, "and you're sure as hell not my friend. You're a figment of my over-heated imagination."

He gave a startled bark of laughter. Whoever and whatever she was, she had the ridiculous ability to make him hover between laughter and outrage. No woman had ever managed that before. She was too damned good at keeping him off balance. Was that her purpose—and Perry's?

To hell with that. If there was anything to his suspicions, he'd learn soon enough.

"So," he said, "you don't think I'm real?" He took one long step, closing the gap between them, and felt her shudder as his chest brushed hers. He could feel the little tips of her breasts, hardening through the shirt. He felt an unexpected hardening in his own body. "What proof do you need, eh?"

She tried to step back, but the temple wall was behind her. "You . . . uh . . ." She thrust out her jaw and glared. "Let me by. I'm going back to the ruins."

"If I'm not real, Mac, you should have no difficulty walking through me."

Suddenly she chuckled. The sound had a hysterical edge. "Great idea," she said. With the full force of her slender weight she pushed against him. The assault drove him back a pace. She stepped to the side, strode to the rim of the temple platform, and slid her foot over the edge.

He caught her arm just as an ancient stone step gave way under her foot. "Are you so eager to break your neck?" he snapped. "Or are you more afraid of something else?"

Her eyes were wide and dark and surprisingly large, rimmed with thick lashes he hadn't noticed before. There was a slight trembling to the lids and at the corners of her lips, as if she'd realized how easy it would have been to tumble down that steep incline in her reckless attempt to escape.

Escape *him*. Was that what she was trying to do?

From the delightful, passionate voice of

Adrienne deWolfe

author of *Texas Outlaw* and *Texas Lover*
comes

TEXAS WILDCAT

*Bailey McShane has had a crush on Zack Rawlins
since she was thirteen and he was courting her
cousin. Now, nearly ten years later, she and Zack
hardly seem able to exchange a civil word with
each other. Bailey knows that is partly due to a
severe drought in Texas, which has been setting
sheepherders—like herself—against cattle
ranchers—like Zack. But Bailey is sure she and
Zack can at least be friends; so when he comes to
her ranch one day with a peace offering, she
gladly invites him to stay for dinner—a dinner
that ends with them both drinking too much
moonshine as a storm gathers overhead. . . .*

"Rain," Bailey whispered.

She jumped to her feet and ran a bit unsteadily to the
window, planting her hands on the sill and sticking her
head and shoulders outside. When she turned her face
to the skies, wind kicked up her sheaf of hair, and thunder crashed like two colliding locomotives, shaking the
wooden frame around her. She giggled like a child.

"Rain!" she shouted, turning to face Zack, her cheeks
streaked by the droplets that were sliding into her collar.
"Let's go watch!"

Before he could draw breath enough to answer, she
grabbed the room's lone lamp and raced into the pitch
blackness of the hallway.

Thrown into darkness, Zack muttered an oath, not waiting for his eyes to grow accustomed before he pushed back his chair. The moonshine hit him full force then, and his knees wobbled. The very idea that some slip of a sheepherder was holding her liquor better than he was was enough to make the blood rush to his head. He grabbed his hat and fanned his face.

"C'mon, Zack!"

Her voice floated in to him above the banging of the front door, and he grinned. He couldn't help it. Rain, by God. There was actually rain!

Draping his Stetson haphazardly over his brow, he hurried across the unfamiliar floor, banging his shin on the doorstop and stubbing his toe on a sitting-room chair. He hardly noticed, though. He was too eager to follow that beckoning light to the circle of brightness it cast on the parched and withered yard. Bailey had balanced the lamp on the porch railing, and when he pushed open the bottom half of the door, he spied her dancing in its yellow blaze. Laughing, she spun like a top, her arms outstretched, her face turned to the heavens. He stumbled to a halt, simply staring.

Her exuberance had loosed her hair from its leather thong, and it whipped around her like slick amber tongues, twining around her upper arms, slapping her buttocks, caressing her thighs. The rain had plastered her jeans to her skin, and the white cotton of her shirt was growing nigh transparent. He swallowed hard, unable to do the gentlemanly thing, unable to tear his gaze away from that sheer clinging fabric and the feminine peaks and valleys it outlined so faithfully.

She crooked her forefinger at him in a beckoning gesture. "C'mere, cowboy," she said huskily.

"What for?" he drawled, stepping off the porch.

"So I can do . . . *this*!"

Before he could guess her intention, she snatched the Stetson from his head and dashed away, whooping like an Indian in a rain dance.

"Hey!" He couldn't stop himself from laughing. "Give me back my hat, woman!"

"Not unless you catch me first!"

"I'll catch you, all right," he growled, and charged after her.

Her heels clattered on the planks of the bridge. In a flash of lightning, he saw her balanced precariously on the bridge's railless edge. He was just about to rush to her when he heard her gasp. Suddenly she wobbled. Her arms and legs flailed. In the next instant she was toppling, shrieking at the top of her lungs.

"Bailey!"

Without thought for his boots or spurs, Zack ran for the stream bank. Slipping and sliding, he scrambled through the rain-slickened reeds and plunged into the water. All he could think in that terrible, mind-numbing moment was that he'd lost her. He'd lost his precious Bailey.

Then he heard a splash.

It was followed by a giggle.

A shadow rose before him, slipping water in cascades, dumping another hatful over itself when it crammed the Stetson onto its head.

"That was fun!" the shadow shouted cheerfully.

Well, that was it. The final straw. Zack grabbed her arm, which threw them both off balance, and they landed side by side in about two feet of water. With a feral sound that was half frustration and half mirth, he fastened his lips over hers, drawing her tongue deep into his mouth. With a hunger he hadn't realized he possessed, he tasted and feasted, plundering the hot, wet mystery behind her breaths. His craving grew more insistent, more demanding with each intoxicating moment.

"Bailey," he groaned, struggling to remember his code of honor, struggling to beat back the desire that crackled along his electrified nerves. "We have to . . . You need to . . . It's time you dried off."

He boosted her to her feet, then hoisted her into his arms.

"Where are you taking me?" she asked, sounding childlike and uncertain as he waded toward the reeds.

"Inside, out of the rain."

"What for?"

"So you can change your wet clothes."

She seemed to think about that for a moment, worrying her bottom lip. Then she loosed a dreamy sigh and dropped her head against his shoulder. "Good. I always wanted you to be the one, Zack. . . ."

From the *New York Times* bestselling
author of **Montana Sky**

NORA ROBERTS

creates a classic suspense tale of a father's
betrayal and a daughter's quest for

SWEET REVENGE

Now available in paperback

The child of a fabled Hollywood star and a
charming, titled playboy, Princess Adrianne
lives a life most people would envy. But her
pampered-rich-girl pose is a ruse . . . a
carefully calculated effort to hide a dangerous
truth. For ten years, Adrianne has lived for
revenge. As a child, she could only watch the
cruelty hidden behind the facade of her parents' fairy-tale marriage. Now, though nothing will bring her mother back, Adrianne is
ready to make her father pay. As the infa-
mous jewel thief, The Shadow, Adrianne is
poised to steal the Sun and Moon—a neck-
lace beyond price—and to taste the sweetness
of her long-sought revenge . . . until she
meets a man who seems to divine her every
secret—and has his own private reasons for
getting close to Princess Adrianne.

On sale in June

TOUCH OF ENCHANTMENT
by Teresa Medeiros

REMEMBER THE TIME
by Annette Reynolds

PUBLIC SECRETS
by Nora Roberts